# THE TWELVE SUSPECTS OF CHRISTMAS

## CHRISTMAS

### PROVENCE COZY MYSTERIES

ANA T. DREW

# CONTENTS

# FREE RECIPE BOOK

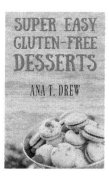

Sign up for my **monthly newsletter** and receive a **free cookbook** in your inbox!

The quick and easy gluten-free recipes in it include:

- macarons
- cookies
- brownies
- tiramisu
- fritters
- puddings

and more!

To sign up, type this url into your browser:
ana-drew.com/patissier

# CHAPTER 1

On the doorstep of Rose's house, Annie smooths out her coat and straightens her scarf before gripping her cane again.

*Hi, I'm Annie. I need your help with a delicate matter.*

As she rolls her opening line over her tongue once more, anxiety curls into a knot in her stomach.

*Is it good?*

*No, it's not. It's sloppy.*

But for the life of her, she can't remember the much better version she'd rehearsed on her bus ride from Cassis to Beldoc.

*Why didn't I write it down!*

With her hand over the doorbell, Annie considers a different approach. Maybe it's not a good idea to ask for help without explaining the specifics first. She could say she has something she'd like to discuss with Rose and leave the details for later.

Alternatively, she could go for extra specific by stating she's Gabriel's grandmother, and she'd like to hire Rose to do some investigating for her. She'd make it clear she knows that

Gabriel is dating Rose's granddaughter Julie and that Rose is training to be a private eye.

*Yes, that's a better introduction.* She will establish a rapport and motivate Rose from the get-go.

Nodding to herself, Annie tucks a loose strand of white hair back into her bun. She takes a deep breath. With a trembling hand, she rings the doorbell. A dog's bark echoes from inside. It startles Annie, amplifying her agitation.

But she's fully committed. There is no turning back.

The door swings open to reveal a graceful woman. She must be Rose. Annie knew Julie's grandmother was full of energy beyond her years, but she hadn't expected just how youthful Rose would be. For some reason, this annoys Annie.

A furry pup resembling a spaniel, but smaller, sniffs her feet.

Rose ushers Annie inside. "You're here for the class? Be quick when you change. You've already missed the breathing routine and neck stretches."

Annie finds herself unable to get a word out.

Rose's eyes linger on Annie's stooped posture and her cane. "Have you done doga or yoga before?"

"I didn't come for the class," Annie finally manages.

"For what, then?"

"My name is Annie Malian. I'm Gabriel's grandmother, and I have something I'd like to discuss with you," Annie says, unsure if this is the intro she'd settled on.

Rose gestures to a door on the other side of the entryway. "Can you wait until the class is over?"

Annie can almost hear the unspoken *Why didn't you call first?* in her tone.

A fair question, for sure. Good thing Rose didn't ask it out loud! All Annie would be able to say is that she's even less at ease on the phone than she is in person with someone she's never met.

Annie hands over her coat and follows Rose into a spacious, sun-drenched verandah that doubles as a doga studio. Julie has explained to Annie that doga is a form of yoga that people practice together with their dogs. Now that Annie has seen Rose, it seems fitting that she'd teach doga.

A handful of students, their dogs of assorted sizes and breeds at their sides, are in the middle of a pose. The room hums with the recorded meditation music and the rustle of movement, punctuated by the occasional bark. The scent of incense wafts through the air, covering up the faint musk of dogs and humans.

Rose directs Annie to a rocking chair in the corner and returns to her mat and faces the students.

Careful to spare the aching joints in her left knee, Annie lowers herself into the chair, sets her purse on her lap and hooks her cane onto the armrest.

She looks around. A veritable sunroom bathed in the gentle winter light of Provence, Rose's verandah looks like a photo from a glossy magazine. Its wraparound windows offer a panoramic view of the garden. *And what a lovely garden that is!* Annie begrudgingly admits. Even nicer than hers in Cassis. Tall fruit trees, their branches bare at this time of year, are artfully interspersed with shorter olive trees. The latter have a rich green foliage and thick trunks gnarled with age.

*A bit like me.*

Annie glances at Rose, a picture of youthful agility in her stretchy yoga outfit. Rose twists her slender and toned body into a pose which she names using a long Hindi term. Annie used to be lithe, too, but that was sixty years ago, before her pregnancies. Rose is a mother and grandmother like Annie and must be in her seventies by now. It feels unfair that Time has been so exceptionally kind to her.

On the other hand, Annie's workout routine for the past ten years has consisted of knitting in front of the TV. Even the gardening, which she used to do daily, has now been fully delegated to her oldest, Claire.

*Shame on you, Annie!*

Closing her eyes, she thanks God that she's still alive and asks him to forgive her for her bout of envy.

With the prayer chasing away the feeling of resentment, Annie reopens her eyes and studies the sunroom once more. The uneven terracotta tiles on the floor must date from when the house was built. Worn rugs cover the central part of the space. Wicker furniture, pushed to the sides to make room for the students, adds a rustic charm to the ensemble.

Annie shifts her attention to the humans and their dogs. The students' faces are flushed with exertion as they follow Rose's instructions as best they can. Some of their dogs try to mirror their movements with varying degrees of success. Two or three roam around and sniff things, people, and other dogs. A pug is fast asleep. His snoring splices a comical note into the new agey soundtrack of the class.

Rose guides her students to lie flat on their backs with their arms by their sides, palms down. They lift their legs and hips off the ground, supporting their lower back with their hands, and bring their feet toward their head.

"*Halasana,*" Rose says. "The plow pose."

Annie goggles and quickly averts her gaze when Rose, still in that rather indecent posture, spreads her legs wide.

*There are men in the room!*

The students follow Rose's lead. After a few seconds, Rose instructs them to fold their legs, hug their knees, tuck their chins into their chest and rock back and forth.

"*Pawanmuktasana,*" she says as her dog licks her face.

Annie winces, fighting back the urge to squirt the sanitizer in her purse onto her own face, and rub.

*How unhygienic!*

"*Pawanmuktasana*    massages    your    internal    organs, releasing trapped gases and improving digestion," Rose preaches before winking. "It's called the gas release pose for a reason."

Right on cue, one of her students farts audibly.

"Well done, Marie-Jo!" Rose praises her.

The woman—an elegant fifty-something—grins back, looking pleased with herself. Annie shifts in her seat, increasingly uncomfortable. She'd love to release some of her own trapped gases right now, but she'd never do it in public. And even if she did, it would be because she couldn't help it, but she'd never act like it were an achievement!

Half an hour later, the lesson draws to a close. Rose guides her students through another sun salutation sequence, part of which is a pose called *downward dog*. The dogs, their tails wagging lazily, seem to be looking down on the efforts of their humans. After all, they've been doing downward dog since the day they were born! And they don't need yoga to be able to lick themselves in ways humans can only dream of.

*Oh dear!* If an hour around Rose results in such inappropriate thoughts, what will Annie become after the joint trip to Picardie she plans to propose to Rose? Will she turn into a tattooed nudist? A green-haired climate protester? A smelly punk?

It took Annie months to come to terms with her youngest grandson's *homosexuality*, which she'd learned about last Christmas. She isn't ready for more disruption in her life just yet.

Perhaps Rose will turn down the offer.

Or maybe Annie will manage to tame Rose into someone more like her, someone who acts her age.

*But the most likely outcome?* They'll cut the trip short, unable to stand each other, and go back separately.

*Was coming to Beldoc a mistake?* Should she apologize for the intrusion and get the hell out of here while she can?

Annie leans on her cane to climb out of the rocking chair when an image flashes before her mind's eye. It's a handsome blue-eyed man, smiling brightly at her. *René*. Young, full of dreams and ideas, hopelessly romantic. Annie's first love. The sweetest and most tragic love of her life. The man whose death devastated his family and broke Annie's heart.

It happened over sixty years ago. But it feels like yesterday because the wound never healed.

With a sigh, Annie sinks back into the chair.

*I'm going to see this through.*

The anticlimactic finale of the class is marked by something called the *corpse pose*, which would be within reach even for Annie. When it's over, the participants exchange an Indian farewell. The students roll up their mats, pet their dogs and share knowing smiles with their teacher and one another.

Rose comes up to Annie, smiling with polite curiosity. "I hope you weren't too bored."

"Oh no," Annie protests. "I was entertained."

"I assume this is about our grandchildren?"

"Not at all."

Rose's eyebrows shoot up.

*Time for some detail.*

"I heard about your new career as a private investigator," Annie says. "I have a case that needs investigating, and I wonder if you'd be interested in taking it on."

"We shall have tea!" Rose exclaims, leaving Annie in a daze.

# CHAPTER 2

*a*fter seeing her last student out, Rose invites Annie into her colorful, messy kitchen.

As Annie takes a seat at the table, Rose asks, "Chai, green, or mint?"

"Chai, please."

Rose prepares the fragrant tea and pours it into two mugs. Annie lifts her chai to her lips. The blended smell of cinnamon, cardamom, and all the other spices that compose the beverage fills up her nostrils.

*Delicious! But too hot.*

She sets the mug down on the table and levels her gaze with Rose's. "It's cold."

Rose's head jerks back. "The tea?"

"No, my case," Annie says. "A suicide has been troubling me for decades. But there's been a recent development." She pauses, looking for the right words.

"Decades." Rose narrows her eyes. "How *cold* are we talking about?"

"1961."

"*Oh là là!*" Waving her hand, Rose leans on the back of her chair. "That's long before I was born."

Annie sizes her up, doing some mental math. Julie is thirty-two, and Rose is her grandmother. Even if Julie's mother had her young, and Rose had Julie's mother young, that still makes her in her seventies. Annie opens her mouth to voice her observation and then bites her tongue. She *needs* something from Rose. Rubbing the woman's face in her shameless lying about her age might prove counterproductive.

"Whose suicide do you want me to look into?" Rose asks. "A family member? A friend?"

"He was my fiancé."

"Well, then." Rose winks at Annie. "You just solved your case!"

"What do you mean?"

Rose stares at Annie, her mischievous smile slipping.

A lump forms in Annie's throat as she catches Rose's drift.

Rose grabs her hand. "It was a bad, insensitive joke, Annie, darling! I'm so sorry."

"We loved each other," Annie says, withdrawing her hand.

Rose fidgets, studying Annie's face with a mixture of regret and sympathy. "I'm sorry he killed himself. Truly."

"He didn't kill himself."

"I'm so silly!" Rose exclaims. "That's why you're here. You believe he was killed."

"That's right."

"I'm listening."

"René Chantome," Annie begins, "was twenty-one and a student at Sciences Po in Paris. In the early days of 1961, he was accused of murdering his roommate, Grégoire Lacaze. He was about to be arrested when he allegedly killed himself."

"What makes you think he didn't?"

Annie gazes at the objects on the shelves without seeing

them. "Several things. One, he hadn't killed Grégoire, and I'll explain why. Two, he hadn't called or written me before he allegedly committed suicide. Three—"

"Sorry to be mean again," Rose interrupts her, "but regarding your second point, have you considered that you hadn't meant as much to him as he had to you? How long had you known each other?"

"Three years, since his parents hired me as a maid in their Marseilles mansion. René, only a year on me, was finishing high school at the time. I'd quit at fifteen so I could work."

"A maid?" Rose hikes an eyebrow. "Were the Chantomes rich?"

"René's father, Pierre-François, owned a flourishing auction house."

Rose nods. "So, the heir and the maid fall in love. How romantic!"

"A second son," Annie corrects her. "René was an idealistic young man, passionate about social justice and other progressive ideas floating around at the time."

"Weren't we all?"

*I just wanted to marry for love and have children.*

"In Paris," Annie continues, "René joined a political movement called the Party of Radical Anti-Capitalists, or PRAC for short."

"I remember PRAC! But not from anything recent."

"They fizzled out in the eighties."

"Were René's parents OK with your relationship?" Rose asks.

"They didn't know about it, nor did his siblings."

"His idea your yours?"

"Mine," Annie says. "I'd insisted that we keep it secret until he finished his studies and the military service. Then we'd get married."

"Oh, yeah, those were the days of mandatory military service for the boys!"

"We were going to live in Paris," Annie carries on. "We were both going to work, so it wouldn't have mattered if his parents disapproved of our match."

"All right, what's your third reason for not buying René's suicide?"

"It never made sense to me that he'd opened his wrists and bled out in the bathtub," Annie explains. "You see, René couldn't stand the sight of blood. If he'd really killed himself, he would've jumped to his death or hanged himself or taken poison... But he wouldn't have opened his wrists."

"Was there an investigation? Did the police have doubts for the same reasons as you?"

"The police found no signs of a struggle," Annie says. "Given that René was facing murder charges and that they found a suicide note in his handwriting, it was an open-and-shut case."

Rose leans forward with a quizzical look on her face. "And the recent development you mentioned? What was it?"

"Two days ago, I received a letter from Olivia Chantome, René's niece. It contained a postcard René must have written me in the first days of January '61, after he returned to Paris from his Christmas break in Marseilles and before Grégoire's murder on January 4."

"What did the postcard say?"

Annie smiles softly. "The first paragraph wished me a merry Armenian Orthodox Christmas, which is on January 6."

"I'm guessing he never mailed that postcard?"

"No. In her accompanying letter, Olivia writes that she found the postcard in a box of her great-uncle's things when she was going through some old junk in the attic."

10

"Was René's second paragraph a McAfee note?" Rose asks.

"What's a McAfee note?"

"A few years ago, the founder of McAfee Antivirus, John McAfee, tweeted from prison 'If I suicide myself, I didn't. I was whacked.' "

"Did he suicide himself?" Annie asks.

"According to the prison authorities, he did."

After digesting that bit of info, Annie answers Rose's earlier question, "No, René's second paragraph wasn't a McAfee note. It was about how he missed me already and couldn't wait to see me again at Easter."

"I see."

"Do you?" Annie searches Rose's face. "I always doubted René's suicide. But after reading those words, I'm convinced he didn't kill himself."

"There's a flaw in your logic," Rose points out smugly.

"Tell me."

"If René wrote the postcard before killing his roommate, then the two aren't mutually exclusive," Rose says. "He might've very well been looking forward to seeing you at Easter. But the murder he committed changed everything."

Annie stares at her, crushed by the injustice of what had happened to René and saddened by Rose's skepticism.

Suddenly, Rose's eyes widen. "It was 1961! We hadn't abolished the death penalty yet. René's head might've rolled at the guillotine."

"René didn't kill Grégoire!" Annie screams. "He had been framed."

"You loved him. Your judgment—"

"This isn't about my judgment," Annie cuts in. "The motive for the murder was supposed to be passionate love and jealousy over Bernadette, a female student Grégoire was dating. Except René was never interested in her romantically. Never!"

"Because he was with you."

"Yes." Annie purses her lips. "I know what you're thinking. René could've been two-timing me. But he wasn't! His heart was pure. I'll eat my cane if it turns out he did."

Rose looks at Annie's cane, wincing. "Maybe if you cook it for a day or two... Still, it's lacquered. That stuff is toxic if ingested."

Frustrated, Annie turns away.

"I'm sorry," Rose apologizes again. "I'm not normally this callous. Someone has cut loose my inner hellcat."

Annie doesn't react to that comment, but she has a suspicion that the scandalized, judgmental looks she threw Rose during the doga class may have something to do with Rose's present cattiness.

"René's killer must've been someone he knew," she says, acting as if they'd agreed that René was innocent.

"Because the police didn't find any defensive wounds?"

Annie nods. "The killer or killers could've used chloroform to render him unconscious, placed him in the bathtub, opened his wrists, and wrote the suicide note."

"Did the police run toxicological and graphological tests at the time?"

"To my knowledge, no toxicological screening was done," Annie says. "Besides, chloroform metabolizes very fast. They wouldn't have detected it back in '61."

"And the graphological analysis?"

"The note was so short it was easy to fake."

Rose cocks her head. "What did it say?"

"One word—*Sorry*. Like I said, easy to fake."

"Hmm..." Rose looks down at her mug before lifting her eyes to Annie. "You've given this quite a bit of thought, haven't you?"

"I've had over half a century to ponder it."

They finish their tea in silence.

Rose sets her empty mug on the table. "I don't have my license yet, which means it would be illegal for me to work for you. I'm afraid you can't hire me."

"Then help me free of charge."

Rose arches an eyebrow. "Do I look like someone who works for free?"

"I know you've helped Julie on several cases with no compensation."

"I did," Rose admits. "And I won't do it again. That is precisely the reason I enrolled in an online program, to be able to charge for my efforts."

"I can offer something nonmonetary in return."

"What?"

"A round trip to Picardie and a stay in the lovely seaside village of Le Crotoy. And also..." Annie wills herself to think quickly. "My profound gratitude. And a chance to clear a good man's name!"

"That last argument would work on Julie," Rose says. "I'm not her, as you may have noticed."

She folds her arms, and waits.

But instead of offering another reason, Annie shrugs, suddenly exhausted. "Well, that's it. That's all I've got."

Neither of them speaks for a long, loaded moment.

Finally, Annie breaks the silence, "Are you in, or should I look for a PI who already has her license?"

"You could always try Julie," Rose suggests. "Or your own grandson. He's a cop, after all, a captain of the Gendarmerie Nationale."

"Julie is busy with her pastry shop, and Gabriel needs to focus on his own cases, if he is to get promoted to commandant anytime soon."

"An established PI will charge you a fortune." Rose chews

on her bottom lip. "Are you prepared to sacrifice your life's savings?"

Annie waves dismissively. "Ah, it can't be that bad."

"Yes, it can. It's what I would charge for a case as cold and hopeless as yours if I already had the license."

"Well, you don't have it, and you won't work for free, so..." With a sigh, Annie grabs the armrests of her chair.

"This means a lot to you, huh?"

Annie heaves herself up. "I wouldn't be here if it didn't. Thank you for the tea."

"Give me a day to think about it," Rose says, leading Annie to the door. "The answer will likely be no, but I'd rather not give it to you in such a flippant mood."

# CHAPTER 3

$\mathcal{R}$ose navigates her car through the quiet streets of Beldoc. The infuriatingly low speed limit of 20 kilometers per hour introduced in August by the mayor, Victor Jacquet, is no issue this morning. She's looking for someone, so she drives way below the limit.

The rush hour has passed, leaving behind a calm that matches the chill in the air. Rose enters the historic center of the town. It looks a bit sad despite the Christmas decorations. In the drizzle, the sun barely illuminates the old stone buildings and casts a faint glow on the wet cobblestones beneath the wheels.

With her King Charles spaniel Lady in the passenger seat, Rose has been driving around for an hour and scanning the familiar landmarks for one middle-aged man—Karl.

That isn't his real name. Someone gave Beldoc's resident tramp that nickname years ago, and it stuck. He does look like a scruffy Karl Lagerfeld. He keeps his long white hair tied in a low ponytail and wears a black leather jacket in almost any weather. Karl saved Julie's life last year, but even she doesn't know his real name. No one does. It is also unclear why Karl has been living on the streets since he set foot in Beldoc. He doesn't like to talk about himself.

Normally at this time of day, the hobo and his faithful mongrel Harley would be hanging out in the town's historic center around the *Place de la mairie* or on rue de l'Andouillette, where the shopkeepers would give them something to eat and drink. Two weeks ago, Julie filled out paperwork to get Karl and Harley beds in a hotel that had been converted into a shelter for the homeless. Rose, being on the municipal council, petitioned Mayor Jacquet. Karl is expecting a reply by today, and Rose is curious to know if Julie's and her efforts bore fruit.

After finding that Karl isn't in the old town, Rose turns toward the riverfront. Something catches her attention under one of the bridges over the Rhône. A human silhouette huddles beneath a blanket in the frigid air. A dog nestles against the human.

*It's got to be them!*

She pulls her Nissan over to the side of the road, grabs Lady, and cautiously descends the wet stone stairs to the underbelly of the bridge. As she approaches the pair, there's no doubt that it's Karl and Harley. But Karl's blanket and Harley's well-worn body warmer are no match for the biting wind. Thank God it isn't the mighty mistral, but it's bad enough.

When she reaches Karl, Rose hunkers down by his side and holds Lady in her lap.

Karl smiles through chattering teeth. "Bonjour, Rose!"

"Bonjour, my friend!" She pets the scruffy mongrel. "Good boy, Harley."

"Everything OK?" Karl asks.

"I'm fine." She looks him up and down. "You, on the other hand..."

"I had a rough night, that's all," he claims in a voice that sounds coarser than usual.

*A sore throat? A cold?* She notices the reddened tip of his nose, the pallor of the rest of his face, the way he's shivering.

"May I?"

Karl protests but Rose is already pressing a palm to his forehead. He's warm. Not burning up, but definitely higher than normal.

"Why are you here when you're sick?" she asks, her voice heavy with concern. "Why aren't you in the squat or in the homeless shelter? Did you hear from Victor about the hotel beds?"

"I was kicked out of the squat by some young newcomers."

"And the shelter?"

Karl shakes his head. "It's full, as always."

"And the new one, the converted hotel?"

"I saw *le maire* yesterday afternoon," Karl pauses to cough into his elbow. "Unfortunately, he said the new shelter won't take Harley and me."

"Why? Do they have a no-dogs policy?"

"No." He hesitates, visibly ill at ease. "They don't think my name is Karl Lagerfeld."

*Oh dear.* "Is that what Julie put on the form."

He nods.

Rose smiles softly. "Will you tell me what your real name is? Do you have any ID?"

He shakes his head, eyes downcast. "Karl is fine. I'm happy with Karl."

*Stubborn man!*

"OK, we'll see about that later," Rose says. "Right now, we need to get you warm, my friend."

He shrugs as if to remind her he's out of options.

Her decision made, she lowers Lady to the ground. "My place. You'll catch pneumonia if you spend another *rough* night outside."

"I'll be all right," Karl argues, but his voice lacks conviction, and his face brightens perceptibly.

After sticking his backpack in the trunk, she helps him into her two-seater. Karl slides the seat as far as it will go, so that Harley can squeeze in at his feet while Lady settles on his knees. During the short drive, Rose calls her family doctor on the hands-free and arranges for a house call that afternoon.

Ten minutes later, Rose leads Karl and Harley to her guest room. Settling Karl on the bed, she tucks a warm blanket around him and heads to the kitchen to make him some tea.

When she returns with a loaded tray, she tries not to pinch her nose. The room is going to need serious airing and cleaning after these two guests are gone. *Oh well.*

"I'll be back in two hours," she says to Karl. "In the meantime, Sarah will come by to check on you. Remember Sarah, my friend and neighbor?"

He grins. "Harley loves Baxter!"

Baxter is Sarah's pug. Last year, when Karl was in the hospital and Harley spent a week at Rose's, he taught Baxter, who'd always peed like a girl, to lift his leg. Since then, the pair have developed a bit of a bromance, perhaps to console themselves after being snubbed by Lady.

Before heading into the old town again, Rose steps across the street to Sarah's.

"It's Karl's lucky day," Sarah announces. "I'm making shortbread."

Sarah is British, though she's lived in Provence most of her life now. She loves that Karl loves everything Anglo-Saxon—especially, shortbread, the Beatles, and Harley-Davidson.

"Keep some for me!" Rose shouts on her way out.

Sarah's shortbread isn't nearly as good as Julie's, but it's infinitely better than anything Rose can bake, which—not counting the store-bought quiche base—is tantamount to nothing.

# CHAPTER 4

$\mathscr{B}$ack in central Beldoc, Rose parks her Nissan in front of Julie's pâtisserie. She picks up Lady so that the spaniel won't get her paws and belly dirty from the wet pavement.

Before heading into Julie's shop, Rose beelines to the festive Christmas window display. Julie and Eric must've put it up last night or early this morning. It's a welcome sight. Garlands of holly with deep green leaves and red berries are draped across the window. Like last year, festoons of silver and gold tinsel shimmer in alluring splendor. But the giant and delightfully whimsical *bûche de Noël* that was the showstopper of the last holiday season is nowhere in sight.

The theme this year is the Thirteen Desserts of Christmas, a Provençal tradition. Rose tries to spot each of the thirteen desserts all meticulously crafted and nestled amid holiday decorations.

The colorful marzipan *calissons* jump out at once.

Rose's eyes trace the path of twinkling fairy lights that illuminates the almonds, hazelnuts, and walnuts in a soft glow. The dates are tucked under a miniature Christmas tree.

Sprigs of mistletoe frame the black-and-white nougats, glazed chestnuts, and sweet olive oil brioches. The glow of a romantic lantern enhances the natural beauty of the fresh fruit and the orangette—candied orange peel coated with dark chocolate.

*Do we have all thirteen?* Rose isn't sure. But, regardless, it's such a lovely display!

Her heart swells with pride. The only culinarily gifted Tassy-Cavallo in three generations, the little girl with chocolate-smeared cheeks, has achieved so much since graduating from Le Cordon Bleu! This display, the shop itself, and the confections inside are works of art. They are the masterpieces that Julie molds day in and day out from gluten-free flour and natural sugar substitutes with unpronounceable names.

Peering through the decorations, Rose spots Flo, the youngest of her four granddaughters, behind the counter. Flo has been Julie's part-time sales assistant since the opening of the shop. Julie and her sous chef Eric must be in the kitchen, baking.

Two and a half years ago, freshly back in Provence, Julie called her kitchen "the lab." That's how the chefs and sous chefs in the grand Parisian *maison* where she used to work referred to their kitchen. But that slip of the tongue grew rarer as Paris gradually seeped out of Julie, and Provence retook its rightful place.

Rose smiles to herself. Even if Julie no longer calls her kitchen a lab, she's still a modern-day alchemist. In fact, she should call it her studio because she's an artist. She's the Salvador Dali of pâtisserie.

*I'm serious!*

Rose pushes open the entrance door. The bell above jingles, announcing her arrival. As she steps in, the smell of baked goods jazzed up with Christmas spice and enhanced with chocolate makes her mouth water.

"*Salut*, Grandma!" Flo greets her. "Can I get you something?"

She's still with a customer, so Rose just blows her a kiss. "I'll wait until the morning rush is over."

Rose sets Lady down and glances at the clock on the wall. In about twenty minutes, things will slow down and remain relatively calm until noon. She'll take advantage of the lull to present her dilemma to the young ones and see if the hive mind has insights to help her decide. Until then she'll just hang out and watch the others work.

A timer dings in the kitchen with a promise of fresh pastries. Rose peeks in. Julie is pulling a tray of macaron shells from the oven, and her sous chef Eric is kneading dough. Rose waves hello without letting an excited Lady cross the threshold. Technically, Lady isn't supposed to be in the front shop either. But only the depressing multinational chains and the cruddiest junk food joints enforce that rule. The nice places that make good food happen to welcome dogs.

*A coincidence?*

With a smug smile on her lips, Rose scratches Lady behind the ears.

*I think not!*

After a quarter of an hour of customers ordering, the doorbell chiming and the cash register humming, the pace slows down. Julie comes out of the kitchen, wearing her toque and chef's uniform, her hands dusted with flour. She pets Lady before washing her hands.

Eric emerges next and grins at Rose. "Madame Tassy! What brings you here?"

"I need your advice."

He points at himself, surprised. "Mine?"

"I mean, all of you." She gestures toward the door. "Can we flip the sign to *Closed* for twenty minutes?"

Everybody looks at Julie le big boss.

She picks up a sticky note, writes "Back at 11:20" on it, and locks up the shop.

Four humans and a canine gather around one of the bistro tables by the window. Rose recounts Annie's visit yesterday afternoon.

Julie's eyes brighten when she's done. "What a story!"

"Are you inclined to say yes?" Flo asks Rose.

Rose pushes a strand of hair out of her face. "I can't investigate for money yet, and I've sworn off doing it for free."

"That's a valid reason," Eric says.

Rose nods a thank-you. "And it isn't the only one! As the elected Queen of Beldoc, I must represent our town at an event in Paris this month. There's also my online PI course, the doga classes, the municipal council, Sarah's book club, and all the other stuff I do."

"What's the event in Paris?" Flo asks.

"The European Santa Convention," Rose replies. "Victor is covering Adonis's expenses, who goes as Beldoc's Santa, and some of mine. The Queens of Provence Committee is funding the difference."

Disbelief thins Flo's eyes. "The Santa Convention?"

"Madame Tassy has a knack for securing invitations to all kinds of cool events," Eric reminds her, winking at Rose.

"Could it be a trap?" Julie asks her. "Why would Victor, your political adversary, cosponsor your trip to Paris?"

Rose shrugs. "No idea. But I'm not going to snub his offer just because I tried to get Beldoc to fire him."

Two years ago, Rose launched a political movement and ran against Victor for the mayor's seat. He won by a margin so small he's still reeling from the humiliation. Naturally, things have been tense between them since then.

Flo's eyes narrow further still. "What will you do at the Santa Convention?"

"I'll take part in the Queens of Provence side event," Rose says. "Its objective is to feminize the assembly and promote the beauty of Provence."

"That's the coolest brief ever!" Eric exclaims.

Rose pinches her chin. "Maybe by being nice to me, Victor hopes I won't run for mayor again. Maybe it's his way of nudging me to stay out of politics."

"Will you?" Flo asks.

"Only if I find an honest way to make a lot of money fast," Rose replies.

Julie snaps her fingers. "Back to Annie's case, folks! I must reopen the shop soon." She turns to Rose. "Does Gabriel know? He and I could—"

Rose flashes a warning hand. "Stop right there. Annie doesn't want to hear about you or Gabriel getting involved in this. Her fallback solution is to go to a professional PI."

"Then that's what she should do," Flo says. "You just gave us two excellent reasons why you can't take on her case."

Rose fidgets with her rings. "There's a third reason... Annie and I got off on the wrong foot. Having her as a coinvestigator might quickly grow tiresome."

Eric cocks his head. "Do you have a reason to say yes, Madame Tassy? And if so, what would that be?"

The question makes Rose stop and think.

"Curiosity?" Julie suggests. "A chance to repair a major injustice?"

"Those would be your motives, not mine," Rose says.

Flo glances from Julie to Rose. "The distinct possibility that you and Annie have a shared great-grandchild sometime soon?"

Julie shifts uncomfortably, discombobulating Rose.

*Trouble in Paradise?*

"I know! It's the spirit of Christmas," Eric exclaims, no doubt, to diffuse the tension.

Flo scoffs as if he said something silly.

*Except, he didn't.*

In a flash of clarity, Rose realizes that the sous chef nailed it.

With still three weeks to go, the sneaky spirit of Christmas has already been making Rose want to wear ugly sweaters and distribute free hugs. Her self-respect won't let her wear the sweaters, but she's been more generous than usual with her hugs. She's also been spending more time with her granddaughters, both in person and over the phone. In her head, she's been talking to her darling Elise every night. Last but not least, she's been lending a helping hand to any friend around her who needed it.

Funnily enough, doing so hasn't felt like a burden, but a privilege. For example, seeking out Karl this morning and taking him to her house so she can nurse him back to health felt like its own reward, despite all the cleaning she'll have to do once Karl and Harley are gone.

Granted, Annie isn't a friend. Prudish and judgmental, she does rub Rose up the wrong way.

But the spirit of Christmas has already lodged in Rose's heart. For over a week now, it's been skewing her perception. Like a shard of the devil's mirror in *The Snow Queen*—only in reverse—it's been shrinking the indifference while magnifying the love.

And if anything could sway Rose to answer Annie's call, it would be like Eric said, the spirit of Christmas.

# CHAPTER 5

"*Y*ou're very kind," Annie says to the train attendant in a Belle Époque uniform who helped her with her suitcase.

Rose thanks him, too.

"Happy to be of service, Mesdames!" He salutes jokingly before moving on to another passenger in need of assistance.

Annie settles onto the hard wooden bench of the vintage steam train, rests her cane against her leg and releases a deep sigh. Next to her, Rose is peppy, a picture of vitality. By contrast, Annie is running on empty, and they're still thirty minutes away from Le Crotoy! The need to lie down and get some shut-eye is so overwhelming Annie wonders if she can make it to the hotel without falling asleep on her feet.

She considers catnapping during this last leg of their trip, despite the hardness of the seats and the prettiness of the landscape along the Bay of the Somme. But there's something she needs to tell Rose before they reach the hotel.

When Rose called her three days ago to say she was in, Annie could hardly believe her ears. As soon as they hung up, she made phone calls to book their trip and rooms at the hotel

Les Tonneaux. With only two weeks left until the Christmas travel rush, she was lucky to get reasonable rates. That being said, the northern shores aren't as popular with tourists in winter as they are in summer.

The only inconvenience was that Rose and Annie had to travel in different cars for most of the trip, given the late booking.

Early this morning, they met at the high-speed TGV train station in Marseilles, and zoomed to Paris, where they changed to a slower train to Noyelles-sur-Mer. And now, they're riding this vintage steam train along the bay to Le Crotoy. Annie smiles inwardly. An antique train for two antique humans—rather fitting, isn't it? Wisely, she chooses not to make that observation aloud. From what she's seen of Rose so far, calling her "antique" will give the retired PE teacher even more reason to dislike Annie.

*If only we'd gotten off on the right foot last week!*

The steam whistle blows, and the train lurches forward. Mad at herself for antagonizing Rose in Beldoc, Annie stares out the window at the cloudy sky and the fields around. She can't see the water from here, only the marshlands between the fields and the sea. Regardless, it's a beautiful view.

Rose interrupts her contemplation. "These wooden benches are charming, aren't they?"

"I don't know about you, but my old bones were happier on the padded TGV seat," Annie says, shifting in discomfort.

Rose falls silent.

*Good grief, why am I like this?*

All Annie had to do was agree with Rose's conversational icebreaker. After that, the small talk would've been marked as done, and they could move on to discussing the case. But now they need a new icebreaker.

Annie racks her brain for a good minute until she finds something. "Who's dog sitting Lady?"

"My neighbor and best friend, Sarah. And another friend Karl. He's also house-sitting."

"Nice."

One more hiatus follows, accompanied by the rhythmic chugging of the engine, the hissing of the steam, and the swaying of the restored carriage.

Rose breaks the silence. "All right, tell me about the Chantomes. What happened to them after they buried René?"

"The parents and the sister, Monique, were heartbroken. René's father, Pierre-François, sold the auction house, his mansion in Marseilles, and the villa in Cannes—"

"Wow," Rose butts in. "They were seriously rich!"

"Pierre-François, Corinne and their children moved across the country, from the Mediterranean shores to the northern coast. They settled in the village of Le Crotoy in Picardie, where we're headed now."

"Did they offer you a job in Le Crotoy?"

"Yes, as a maid at the hotel," Annie says. "But my parents and friends were all in Marseilles, so I stayed."

"Were you able to find another job?"

"I went to work at a textile factory for a while. When a publisher called Editions Jeanne Laffitte opened in Marseilles, I joined them as a cleaner, then packager, and then binder. And then I retired."

Rose narrows her eyes. "Wait. Rewind. You mentioned a hotel in relation to the Chantomes..."

"Good catch!" Annie smiles coyly. "Pierre-François bought one of the town's oldest hotels, Les Tonneaux."

"And that's where you booked our rooms."

"That's right, Sherlock!" Annie grins.

Rose grins back.

*Did we just trade sincere smiles? Perhaps all is not lost...*

"My understanding is," Annie carries on, "that René's

surviving siblings Monique and Jacques, both in their eighties now, live on the premises. Their children and grandchildren run the hotel."

"Is Olivia, who forwarded you René's postcard, one of them?"

"Yes. She's Monique's granddaughter. I hope we'll meet her and talk to her."

"We're going to talk to all of them." Rose angles her body toward Annie, excited. "It was a very smart move to put us in their hotel!"

*Did she just compliment my intelligence?*

Annie perks up, feeling hopeful for the first time since her botched approach. If they both make an effort to soften their edges, if they can set their likes and dislikes aside, then maybe this investigation isn't doomed. Maybe they can work as a team and uncover the truth about René's death. That's Annie's biggest ambition before she bows out.

The only thing that dampens her spirits right now is how cold it is on this train. Then again, this isn't a replica, but an actual century-old dinosaur that's been resuscitated and put back on rails. One shouldn't be surprised it's unheated.

Rose pulls her pashmina wrap tighter around her shoulders. "Do you know why the Chantomes traded the sunshine of le Midi for the cold? It's the opposite end of the country!"

"I guess they wanted to put as much distance as possible between themselves and everything that reminded them of René."

"Hmm..."

Annie glances at Rose. "You don't seem convinced."

"Honestly, no. It isn't just the distance. They went from the second largest city in France to a village of two thousand. That's a drastic change of lifestyle."

"Maybe they felt it was what they needed."

"Maybe." Rose opens her purse and pulls out a notebook and a pencil. "Give me their names again and who's who."

"Jacques and Monique are René's siblings, both widowed now," Annie begins. "Olivia is Monique's granddaughter. Monique's son and his wife live abroad. Jacques has a daughter Hélène and a grandson, Armand, both involved with the hotel."

"Do you suspect Jacques or Monique of having something to do with René's death?"

Annie drapes her coat over her back to get warmer, but also to carefully consider her reply. "No, I don't."

"Really?" Rose expels a disbelieving snort. "Your face says otherwise."

"It's just a... hunch if you will. I don't have any evidence, nothing at all to support it."

"Hunches are all one often has early on in an investigation."

"Both Corinne and Pierre-François favored René, their younger son," Annie says. "He was handsome, bright, and kind. It was impossible to know him and not to love him."

"Were his siblings jealous?"

"Jacques was, especially after René was admitted to the prestigious Sciences Po school in Paris, where Jacques had tried and failed."

"And the money?" Rose asks. "Splitting the inheritance two ways left Jacques with more than if it had been three ways."

"I don't recall him being greedy. But René's academic success and his being their parents' blue-eyed boy never sat well with Jacques. That I remember."

"All right then, we have ourselves a suspect! His motives for murdering René could be stronger, but one should never underestimate the destructive power of envy."

Annie nods with vigor. "There's a reason it's one of the seven deadly sins."

Rose's stomach rumbles.

"It's past lunchtime," she says. "Do you think we can buy something on this train?"

Annie opens her handbag and pulls out two sandwiches wrapped in foil. "Ham or hummus?"

"You choose," Rose says, her eyes lighting up.

Annie offers her the hummus sandwich. "I thought you might be a vegetarian."

"Yoga and meat aren't incompatible, you know."

Annie withdraws her hand and gives Rose the ham sandwich instead. They chew in silence for a few minutes, gazing at the landscape outside. The train slows down and stops at a tiny place called Morlay halfway between Noyelles sur Mer and Le Crotoy.

"Can you tell me about your late husband?" Rose asks Annie out of the blue. "What was his name?"

"Andre Bogossian."

"Armenian like you?"

Annie nods.

Rose has more questions. "How did you meet him?"

"We'd known each other since we were children. Our parents were friends."

"Was it a love match or an arranged marriage?" Rose asks.

"The former. About two years after René's death, our friendship became something more."

"Were you friends with Andre when you dated René?"

"Yes."

"Did he know about your secret romance?"

"He was the only one in my entourage who did," Annie says. "We were that close."

Rose gives her a loaded stare.

Annie holds her gaze. "What?"

"You know what." Rose swallows the last bite of her sandwich. "What if Andre was in love with you the entire time? What if he suffered atrociously while you were with René?"

"What are you saying, Rose?"

"I'm saying he had a motive."

Annie wipes her fingers with a paper tissue. "Such as?"

"Jealousy, my dear. It's a powerful motive!"

Annie looks at her then throws her head back and gives a hearty laugh.

Rose waits for her to finish. "I totally understand why you find the idea preposterous. Andre was your best friend. Your second big love. The father of your children."

"He was also a very decent human being," Annie says. "Even if we assume he was secretly in love with me while I was with René, he'd never do something as vile as kill René's roommate, frame René for that murder, and then bump off René so that he could have me."

"I hear you, really! All I'm saying, you can't be one hundred percent sure unless he had an ironclad alibi for the first days of January 1961."

"He did."

Rose's head jerks backward. "Oh?"

"He was doing his military service at the time." Annie stifles a smile before adding, "You weren't born yet, so you wouldn't remember, but France was waging a war in Algeria in 1961. That's where Andre was in early January 1961."

"No leave for Christmas?"

"Nope."

"That does sound like an ironclad alibi."

"You don't say," Annie mutters as she settles her gaze on the scenery outside.

# CHAPTER 6

*a* strange mood that Annie can only describe as part excitement, part melancholy comes over her as the old locomotive continues skirting around the Bay of the Somme. She watches the marshlands for a while and then lets her eyelids fall, hoping to power nap for the rest of the way.

But instead of lulling her to sleep, the sway of the car and the clatter of wheels on tracks sends her back in time to a different train journey she made alone many, many years ago, in the spring of 1960.

Annie is on a train from Marseilles to Paris. She's sitting still but her heart is aflutter with a crazy mix of emotions. There's excitement, but also fear. She's taken her Friday and Saturday off. Her strict, deeply conservative Armenian parents don't know that. Nor do they suspect that she's making a round trip to Paris so that she can spend the weekend with René.

This is before the TGV technology "moved" Marseilles five hours closer to Paris, so the journey feels never-ending. Finally, the train pulls into the Gare de Lyon. It's Annie's first time in the capital.

Hesitantly, she steps onto the platform. The hustle and bustle of the crowded station do nothing to calm her agitated nerves. But the moment she spots René waiting for her, all her distress and anxiety fade away. As if on cue, his eyes light up at the sight of her. A big, toothy grin spreads across his face.

Rushing to her, he takes her in his arms. "*Mon amour!*"

She draws away when he moves to kiss her. "What if someone from Marseilles recognizes us?"

"The odds of that happening are ridiculously small," he says, laughing.

But he doesn't try to kiss her again until they reach the cramped apartment he's renting with another student not far from the Gare de Lyon. The student in question, Grégoire, is out with his new girlfriend. René informs Annie that she'll meet them later in the afternoon. He sets her suitcase by the door in his room and kisses her passionately, sensually, the way they'd never kissed before. Annie loves every exhilarating moment of it.

An hour later, they head out.

First, René takes her to the Latin Quarter, which Annie has always wanted to visit. The streets here are alive with such youthful energy and so many fashionable people that Annie can't stop gawking. The young women wear the latest, most daring styles. Annie has seen them on the pages of the fashion magazines in her aunt's hair salon, but rarely on the streets of Marseilles. Her native city suddenly feels very provincial and behind the times.

Here everybody is a fashion icon. The young Parisiennes wear short geometric dresses with oversized buttons and puffed sleeves. Older women are no less stylish in their capri pants and drainpipe jeans. All the females have big, bouffant hair and heavily made-up, winged eyes—not uncommon in Marseilles but worn here with a lot more panache.

As they approach the university buildings, the city begins to feel like a wide shot from an artsy new-wave film.

Place de la Sorbonne is teeming with students. René pulls Annie onto a sidewalk terrace and orders two cups of coffee. While they lounge in the elegant wicker chairs sipping their *petits noirs,* Annie overhears fragments of conversations around them. The students talk about politics and literature. They make plans to build a better world, end colonialism, and emancipate women. The word *new* is on everyone's lips—New Left, new rules, new activism, new wave...

It's all very inspiring. And very intimidating.

From the Latin Quarter, René takes her to Sciences Po, his school. There, they meet up with his gang—René's roommate Grégoire, his pretty girlfriend Bernadette, Bernadette's bestie Marie and a young man whose name escapes Annie now. *Bernard? Baptiste?* Annie decides to go with Baptiste.

In her present, the conductor announces they'll arrive in Le Crotoy in ten minutes. Annie tries to shake the memory and refocus on the here and now, but the past clings to her, refusing to release her.

She's still in Paris, strolling with René and his friends through Le Marais down to Bastille. When they pass the medieval Place des Vosges, Bernadette and Grégoire break away from the group. They claim to have some business they need to address. Marie and Baptiste stay. Annie likes them. All the young people René has introduced to her so far are just as impressive as he is. They're destined to join the ranks of the country's elite and become as influential in twenty years as their parents are now.

For the next few hours, Annie hangs out with René, Marie and Baptiste. When the males get into a heated political discussion on Gaullism versus Communism, Marie is kind enough to point out to Annie the sites they pass, explaining what's what.

"Have you decided which party you're joining?" René asks Marie at one point.

Turning to Annie, he supplies some context, "Marie has been dithering for a while now between the Marxist Situationist International and the Trotskyist Workers' Voice."

"How are they different?" Annie asks. "What do they want?"

Baptiste looks at her like she's a simpleton. "The end of capitalism, of course! Have you ever heard of the workers' rights?"

Annie feels infinitely embarrassed by her ignorance.

Marie bursts out laughing. "Thank you, Annie! I don't see much difference between the two, either, which is why I hesitate. Both are anti-imperialist, internationalist and avant-garde movements."

Annie shoots her a grateful look.

*It's Marie that René should date, not me,* she catches herself thinking.

Crushed by her lack of savvy, Annie glances at René.

He wraps a protective arm around her shoulders. "May I just point out," he says to Baptiste, "that the only actual *worker* among us is my fiancée?"

Baptiste cowers, visibly contrite.

But René isn't ready to let him off the hook yet. "Her family's social condition means that Annie needs to work for a living. That is why she has no time for learning the difference between Marxism and Trotskyism."

Baptiste's face has now turned the color of beetroot. He looks so miserable that Annie is tempted to confess she finds politics mind-numbingly boring. But she feels that such an admission would be disloyal to René who jumped to her rescue.

Her heart floods with tenderness. Deep inside, she knows he's overidealizing her and her family. To him, their poverty is noble, their lives are authentic. That may be so. But what René doesn't realize is that they'd be happy to swap places with his upper-crust parents any day of the week and twice on Sunday.

When Annie and René get back to the apartment, it's past midnight. Grégoire is already asleep in his room. They tiptoe into René's room and kiss for over an hour. Then René offers her his single bed, declaring he'll be happy to sleep on the floor. Annie insists they can fit in it together. And they do without a problem. The real problem turns out to be how to keep their hands and lips off each other.

Annie is perfectly aware that her traditional, patriarchal community expects her to save her "virtue" for the marital bed. Granted, she and René are secretly engaged. She trusts him when he says he plans to marry her after he's finished his studies and mandatory military service. But that's four years away. A lot can happen in the meantime.

As they make out, the voice of reason tells her to stop. René himself is telling her they should stop, and he should go sleep on the floor by the opposite wall.

But one rarely listens to the voice of reason when one is twenty years old and in love.

# CHAPTER 7

*R*ose glances at Annie who seems to have fallen asleep.

*Did she hear the conductor's announcement?*

Gently, she touches the other woman's arm. "We're almost there."

Annie opens her eyes. She looks ruffled but not in the disoriented way people do when they awake from a slumber. It must be her nerves. The prospect of seeing René's siblings again after all those years must be wreaking havoc on her already fragile constitution.

Rose opens her mouth to tell Annie to pull herself together if she wants their investigation to be more than an emotional trip down memory lane. But the turmoil and vulnerability in Annie's eyes make her change her mind.

*Oh well.* What's the chance they'll find out what really happened to René in 1961? Less than 1 percent. Telling Annie she's a mess is unlikely to change that. But it's very likely to vex her.

Their museum piece of a train slows down as it pulls into the cute little station in Le Crotoy. The steam whistle blows one last time, marking the end of their journey. As soon as the car comes to a stop, a commotion erupts as the passengers stand up, exchange excited words, and pick up their luggage.

Rose and Annie put their coats on. While Rose gathers their carry-on suitcases, Annie rises from the hard seat, leaning heavily on her cane and wincing. The helpful steward in period uniform returns to give her a hand. A station agent across the gap helps Annie step down on the platform.

Rose disembarks after her, squinting in the faint gleam of the winter sun.

"How far from here to the hotel Les Tonneaux?" she asks the station agent. "Is it a walking distance?"

"No more than ten minutes." His eyes dart to Annie's cane. "Well, more for madame."

Rose turns to Annie. "I'd love to stretch my legs, and I don't mind rolling both our suitcases. Shall we walk?"

"All right," Annie agrees to her surprise.

Maybe she sees it as a chance to delay the moment that's had her in knots for the past half hour...

"Walk toward the water tower," the agent says, "and continue down to the sea until you see an old mansion that looks like a mini castle. That'll be Les Tonneaux."

Thanking him, Rose grabs a handle in each hand and heads in the direction of the water tower whose tip is visible above the roofs. Annie totters behind her, her cane clicking on the pavement.

The air is fresh and salty, tinged with the scent of seafood from the restaurants they pass. As they get away from the tracks, the town grows prettier by the minute. Charming houses, their façades a patchwork of vibrant colors, line the narrow streets. Some are half-timbered, others brick, and others more recent, but matching the older ones in style and spirit.

There's no denying it, Le Crotoy is just as alluring as

Rose's Provençal hometown Beldoc. In fact, it could've been Beldoc's long-lost twin, lost as a baby and raised in Picardie.

They get to the hotel too quickly for Rose's liking. Nestled by the beach, the red-tinted building with fat, barrel-like turrets, does look like a shrunk castle.

The cozy lobby is quiet except for the occasional creak of the floorboards and the hushed conversation between the receptionist and a client. A muted fragrance of wood and leather from the armchairs and sofas scattered around enhances the sense of comfort.

As they wait, Rose takes in the historic features that have been lovingly preserved. The lofty ceilings are enhanced with ornate plasterwork. Velvet curtains drape the sash on the windows. The uneven wooden beams stretching high between the walls, as well as the sturdy wrought iron pieces—some inlaid and others freestanding—give the place a rustic touch. On two opposing walls, large patches of old stone wall have been stripped of stucco. Somewhat counterintuitively, they accentuate the warm feel of the lobby.

When her client walks away, the receptionist greets Annie and Rose with a friendly smile. "*Bonsoir, mesdames!* Welcome to Les Tonneaux. We have been expecting you."

Rose trades looks with Annie. The receptionist is in her early thirties. *A Chantome?* Could she be Monique's granddaughter Olivia, the one who forwarded René's postcard to Annie?

Rose puts on her glasses to read the name on the receptionist's badge. It says "Diane." None of Chantomes are named Diane in Rose's recollection.

"Thank you," Rose says. "We're delighted to be here. How old is this place?"

"Mid-eighteenth century, madame," Diane answers with pride.

"Are you one of the owners' grandchildren?" Rose asks.

Annie pinches her arm hard.

Rose glares at her. *I'm just doing what you asked me to do, dummy!*

The receptionist chuckles. "No, I'm not. But you'll see them around. They work at the hotel. Armand's mother, Hélène, is the manager."

After making copies of their IDs and registering Annie's bank card, she hands them their room keys. "Breakfast is served on the ground floor, between seven and ten. We also serve dinner."

"Can we book a table?" Rose asks, since Annie seems to have swallowed her tongue.

"I'm afraid we're full for tonight, but I'll put you down for tomorrow."

"That's a shame," Rose says.

Diane's fingers dance over the computer keyboard before she adds, "Tonight is Friday Quiz Night in the bar area. It starts at ten in case you're interested. Olivia and Armand are the quizmasters."

"What's the prize?" Rose asks, hoping that it's money.

"The winning team is invited to dine at the captain's table on Saturday. In case the winner has other plans or checks out, they get a lovely goodie bag."

Annie narrows her eyes. "Who's the captain?"

"Monsieur Jacques Chantome, of course!" The receptionist grins. "He may have withdrawn from the day-to-day business, but he's still the captain of this ship."

The distaste painted on Annie's face at that comment reminds Rose that Annie suspects Jacques of murdering René.

"Monique Chantome co-owns the hotel," the receptionist says, "but she's never been as hands-on as Monsieur Jacques and his daughter Hélène."

Before Annie can open her mouth, Rose claps her hands. "Wonderful! We'll be there."

Annie releases a sigh. "I'll need a nap before we go."

"You'll find your beds very comfortable," Diane boasts.

"At this point, I could sleep on anything," Annie says.

Diane points to her left. "Your rooms are that way, third floor. We had a small elevator installed next to the staircase earlier this year, so you won't have to climb the stairs."

Thanking her, Rose and Annie roll their suitcases to the central staircase illuminated by grand chandeliers. Tucked into its side, the elevator blends well into the historic decor despite its modern look. They ride it to the third floor and step into a narrow hallway with vintage patterned wallpaper, faded floral carpets and dim lighting fixtures. Rose leads the way to their adjacent rooms.

Before they split, they agree that Rose will pick Annie up in two hours at seven-thirty. They'll grab dinner before the quiz.

"I'm going to sleep until then," Annie says.

"Suit yourself. I'll head to the beach. A brisk walk will be just the thing before dinner."

"Perhaps I'll join you tomorrow, provided you don't walk briskly." With that, Annie wobbles to her room.

Rose helps her drag her suitcase inside. White wisps tumble onto her deeply lined face, making Annie appear even more fragile than before. In a few years, a walker will replace the cane. And a few more years after that...

Rose turns away, shocked by the dark turn that her thoughts took. She strides to her own door, feeling at once sad for Annie and proud of herself for having taken much better care of her body.

*I'll still be fit at eighty-four, you'll see! No canes before my one hundredth birthday.*

The door opens to a lovely room overlooking the inner

courtyard. A view of the bay would've been better, but that's all right. Annie had booked at the last minute. They're lucky to have rooms at all.

The interior is complete with a double bed, a wardrobe, two nightstands, a desk, and a chair. A nod to the hotel's rustic-chic vibe, the furniture is antique all right, but it's more functional than opulent. Rose opens her suitcase, transfers her toiletries to the impeccable bathroom, and returns to the main area.

The embroidered bed cover and the throw pillows scattered on the bed look very inviting.

*I'll just check if the bed is as comfortable as Diane said.*

Rose sits down and bounces cautiously, testing the springiness of the mattress. *Hmm...*

She takes off her shoes, puts her feet up and leans on the padded headboard. *Not bad.*

She stretches out. *Niiice!*

Before her conscious mind has a chance to register it, she drifts off to sleep.

## CHAPTER 8

*A*n insistent rapping on the door wakes up Rose.

Someone calls from the other side. "Rose? Are you there?"

With an effort, Rose peels her eyelids apart. It takes her a moment to find her bearings. Once she recalls her hotel room in Le Crotoy and that she fell asleep when she was supposed to be walking briskly on the beach, her mood darkens.

*How did that happen?*

Unlike the frail Annie, Rose wasn't feeling tired or sleepy after their three-leg trip, first on the high-speed TGV, then the regular train, and finally the steam-powered Bay of the Somme train. When she stepped into her room, she was full of energy, ready to put on her walking shoes and head out.

*What the hell happened?*

More knocks interrupt her self-probe, accompanied by the same rusty voice, laced with concern, "Are you there? Are you all right? You were supposed to collect me twenty minutes ago, but you didn't show up."

Rose jackknifes to a sitting position and checks her watch.

It's ten to eight. "I'm here," she calls in a voice hoarse from sleep.

Another knock suggests Annie didn't hear her.

Rose climbs out of bed and pads to the door. "Opening!"

When Annie steps in, she looks much better than two hours ago. She's freshened up, redone her hair and swapped her comfy brown cardigan for a comfy gray cardigan.

"What happened?" she asks Rose.

Frowning, Rose mutters, "I fell asleep."

"The body has its limits at our age," Annie says with a sympathetic smile.

Piqued, Rose juts her chin out. "We're not the same age."

"You're in your seventies, aren't you?"

Reluctant to lie too blatantly, Rose settles for, "It's none of your business."

"All I'm saying is that, even if you're in good shape, being in denial of your age doesn't make you younger."

"Short fox, sour grapes."

Annie does a double take. "I'm sorry?"

"I was referencing a fable."

" 'The Fox and the Grapes' by Aesop," Annie says. "I know."

It's Rose's turn to flinch.

Annie smiles. "Didn't I tell you I worked at a publishing house for thirty years? The jobs I held were manual, but I still got to read quite a bit."

"Well, then, you know what I mean."

Annie crosses her arms. "No, I don't."

"Yes, you do."

*Do I really need to spell it out? You're pouring scorn on what you can't have.*

They stare each other down.

"I'll be ready in ten minutes," Rose says, deciding to let it go.

She motions Annie to the armchair, picks her attire for tonight, and heads to the bathroom. As she takes her clothes off, she rescinds her earlier resolution to treat Annie to dinner.

*We're going dutch,* ma cocotte!

Ten minutes later, Rose has taken a turbo shower, changed into designer jeans and a cashmere turtleneck, and patted in her facial cream. She slips her makeup into her purse to apply it at the restaurant before they return to Les Tonneaux for the quiz.

Annie heaves herself up, and the pair head out of the hotel. They pick the first bistro that has a vacant table for two. Their dinner is a tense affair. Neither Rose nor Annie says much throughout their appetizer and main course. Instead, they stare out the window at the street illuminated by tall lamps and enlivened by Christmas decorations. They skip dessert and pay separately.

The short distance back to the hotel is filled with hostile silence. Out of the corner of her eye, Rose watches Annie lean on her cane, her breaths coming out in labored puffs. Rose puts an extra bounce into her step.

*In your face!*

It's nine forty-five when they enter the bar area at the back of the hotel on the ground floor. It's almost full and uniquely inviting. The first thing Rose notices is the Christmas tree in the corner. Decorated with golden ornaments and glittery tinsel, it sparkles just like a Christmas tree should. From there, her gaze travels to the fireplace. It was empty earlier, but now flames are dancing in it, their warmth offering a respite from the chill outside.

There's lots of dark polished wood and a few antique mirrors, but the chairs are comfortable and the tables modern.

A thirty-something female and a male, both in Santa hats, welcome everyone who comes in. They must be Olivia and her cousin Armand, the emcees of the quiz. But they don't assign tables, letting the guests sit where they want.

Rose spots an empty table for two by the wall. She rushes to it, slaloming between seats, before someone else can grab it for themselves. Annie arrives at the table several minutes later.

After the last empty seats are filled, Armand fingers his phone, and a Christmas carol begins to play softly from hidden speakers. He then picks up a basket and goes around the room, collecting everybody's cell phones and distributing buzzers. He assures the guests they'll recover their phones as soon as the quiz is over.

A waiter moves through the room, his tray laden with drinks, snacks, and pastries ordered by the patrons. A mix of sweet aromas fills the air, adding to the cozy ambiance. The guests chat in hushed tones, their anticipation palpable as they wait for the quiz to start.

Olivia plants herself in the center of the room where everyone can see her.

She clears her throat. "For those new to the Les Tonneaux Quiz Night, you can play in teams of one, two, or three. If you're a bigger group, then you have to split up."

"What's tonight's theme?" someone asks.

"Christmas in literature and poetry." She surveys the room. "Ready? Let the quiz begin!"

Armand takes center stage. Stroking his funky suspenders, he explains the rules of the game. While he speaks, Rose leans forward in her seat. Beside her, Annie adjusts her glasses.

"Are you ready for the first question, Mesdames, Messieurs?" Armand asks, raising his voice.

The teams say they are.

"We'll begin with an easy one." He turns up the volume of

the song that's playing in the background. "Can you name this Christmas carol?"

Several buzzers go off.

Olivia checks her screen. "Team number four buzzed first. Go!"

"Silent Night," a woman from the table next to Rose's says.

"Correct!" Olivia claps her hands, and everyone follows suit. "One point for team four!"

Armand lifts his forefinger. "Two bonus points if you can name the author of the lyrics and the approximate date!"

No one buzzes.

Pulling a disappointed face, Olivia gives the answer, "Joseph Mohr, an Austrian priest, wrote the lyrics in 1816."

Rose turns to Annie. "I knew the title, but I was too slow. Damn! We need to win this quiz so we can dine with the Chantomes."

"Don't I know that?"

"Then focus." Rose turns toward Armand who's preparing to read the next question.

"Who and how," he begins, "defeats the Mouse King in Hoffmann's famed Christmas tale?"

Annie hits the buzzer, but not fast enough.

The guest who beat her to it, declares proudly, "The Nutcracker kills the Mouse King!"

"Does he do it alone?" Olivia asks him. "How does he do it?"

The guest signals that he doesn't know.

Armand turns to Rose and Annie's table. "Let's see if the second buzzer has a more complete answer."

"First, Marie throws a slipper at him," Annie says. "And then the Nutcracker stabs him with a sword."

Olivia gives her a thumbs-up. "Team three earned their first point!"

Next up is a question about an English poem that neither Rose nor Annie is familiar with. Another team gets it right, earning a point.

Armand throws in another question, "What gift does the Little Prince get for Christmas in Antoine de Saint-Exupéry's masterpiece?"

Confused whispers fill the room.

Racking her brain, Rose glances at Annie who reaches for the buzzer. She's the only one, by the way.

"It's a trick question," Annie says. "There is no mention of Christmas gifts in *The Little Prince*."

Her shoulders tensing, Rose waits for the hosts' verdict. Everybody's eyes are on them.

"Correct!" Olivia exclaims. "One more point for team three!"

"Next question isn't a trick, I promise," Armand begins. "Who is the author of the beloved children's book *Babar and Father Christmas* in which an elephant travels from the Elephant Kingdom to Europe to find Father Christmas who hadn't replied to his children's letter?"

Annie's hand doesn't hesitate this time. But another guest with a better reaction time steals her point by giving the right answer—Jean de Brunhoff.

"Coming up a triple question!" Armand raises his hand to command attention. "What powerful magical item does Harry Potter receive during his first Christmas at Hogwarts, from whom and in which book? You must get all three answers right to qualify. The reward is you earn three points!"

As the teams whisper in huddles, Annie turns to Rose. "Harry Potter came out after I retired from the publishing industry. I never got around to reading those books."

Rose hits the buzzer regardless.

Olivia points at her. "Team number three, go!"

"Professor Dumbledore gave Harry the cloak of

invisibility in *Harry Potter and the Philosopher's Stone*," Rose says.

"Aaand..." Olivia pauses for effect. "Three points for team three!"

To Annie's pleasantly surprised look, Rose explains, "I read that book to my great-granddaughter Rania last Christmas."

As the hosts prepare to launch the next question, Rose places her hand over the buzzer without touching it.

Annie frowns. "We'll be disqualified if we buzz for nothing."

"I won't press unless I know the answer or see it in your eyes," Rose says. "Otherwise, we're too slow."

Armand reads out the question, "What misfortune befalls Kai, and how does his friend Gerda help him in Hans Christian Andersen's 'The Snow Queen'?"

Her eyes on Annie, Rose bears down on the buzzer, praying she hasn't misread her teammate's expression. If she has, Rose will answer. She loves that tale, but she fears she'll get the details wrong, mixing up the original story and the various animated versions she's watched with her granddaughters over the years.

"Team three buzzed first." Armand gestures that they can speak.

"Kai gets splinters from a troll's mirror in his heart and eye, which makes him unfeeling," Annie says. "Then the Snow Queen kidnaps him."

She stops as if considering something.

"Will you have a go at the second part of the question?" Olivia asks her.

She nods. "Gerda embarks on a long journey to rescue Kai. Her love and persistence eventually lead her to the Snow Queen's palace, where she finds Kai. Gerda's warm tears break the spell, and Kai becomes himself again."

"Team three is leading with five points!" Olivia exclaims.

Rose mimes tipping a hat off to Annie who leans back in her seat. There's a funny expression on her face. It isn't triumph, pride, or satisfaction as Rose would've expected. It's something deeper, tinged with so much melancholy that Rose's own heart pinches in response.

And, suddenly, she knows. *But of course!* That's what this whole investigation is about—rescuing René.

Granted, Annie's sweetheart is long dead. But the way he went, allegedly after murdering a friend out of jealousy for another woman, makes him as mean as Kai under the spell. And while Annie can't bring René back from the dead, she can rehabilitate him. She's out to salvage his memory, to free the boy she loved from the evil spell.

Rose's annoyance with Annie melts away, at least for now.

As the quiz winds down, Annie and Rose keep their lead, despite not answering any more questions. Luckily for them, no single team managed to get enough correct answers to take the lead.

At eleven, the quiz ends, and the hosts name them as the winners. Everybody applauds.

Rose raises her teacup in a toast. "We secured that dinner. Well done, teammate!"

With eyes sparkling, Annie clinks her cup against Rose's.

# CHAPTER 9

*T*oo excited about the upcoming dinner with the Chantomes, Annie barely slept at night. So, she had to make up for it in the morning. Thankfully, Rose left her alone until lunchtime. They grabbed something to eat in a bistro on the main street, and then Rose dragged Annie to the beach.

"There's nothing like a walk outdoors to boost the mind," she told Annie. "We're going to need our minds at tonight's dinner even more than during the quiz."

Unable to keep up, Annie trudges behind Rose and tells herself she should've known she was in no shape for this. Especially not after a sleepless night. The pristine sandy beach of the bay is sublime. No doubt about it. But Annie's energy is low. Her joints ache and her knee is killing her. And there are no benches anywhere in sight.

*This walk is a mistake. I shouldn't've listened to Rose!*

To distract herself, Annie focuses on the birdlife and then gazes at the sea. She watches it lap at the shore in the foreground before shifting her eyes to the horizon, where the steel gray of the water blends with the overcast sky.

Annie halts and turns around. "I'm heading back to the hotel."

"Already?" Rose backtracks to her.

Annie suppresses a huff of annoyance. "If I keep going, maybe my mind will become all fresh and sharp, but I'll have no legs to take me to the dinner tonight."

With a nod, Rose offers her arm to support Annie in addition to her cane. Grudgingly, Annie accepts it. They return to their rooms in resentful silence, their camaraderie from last night gone without a trace.

Three hours later, Annie follows Rose through the hotel's bustling restaurant. It's overcooled for Annie's liking, and she's worried she isn't dressed warmly enough. Rose pushes open the double doors to the private back room where they're expected. Stepping inside, Annie realizes it's much quieter and warmer in here than in the front room. That means Annie won't have to ask people to repeat what they say, and she won't be shivering throughout the meal.

*Two headaches down, two dozen to go.* The biggest of them is Jacques's and Monique's reaction when they realize who she is. If they haven't already, thanks to Olivia.

Another major concern is the prospect of spending the evening next to Jacques, the man she suspects of being somehow involved in her fiancé's—and his brother's—death. Rose volunteered to do most of the talking, for which Annie is grateful, but still. She fears she'll be too tense, and it will show, ruining Rose's efforts.

To distract herself from her worries she looks around. The twinkle of fine strings of Christmas lights framing the windows gives the room a cozy feel. Both windows overlook the sandy beach and the calm sea glistening in the dark. A large oakwood table dominates the space. Three generations of the Chantome family are already seated around it.

Armand springs up from his seat and ushers Rose and Annie to the chairs reserved for them.

Olivia raises her glass. "Welcome to our quiz winners, Rose and Annie! Ladies, you were amazing!"

Her grandma Monique and Armand's grandpa Jacques are seated on the opposite sides of the table. Time hasn't been kind to Jacques. His once robust frame has shrunk, and his shoulders are hunched as if carrying the weight of the years. His face used to be full of vitality just like René's, but it's now all saggy and wrinkled. And sour.

Monique has aged, too, so much that Annie wouldn't have recognized her. But her eyes still hold a spark, a hint of the flirty, always laughing teenager she was when Annie knew her.

Monique and Jacques stare right back at Annie. They're clearly paying more attention to her than to Rose. *How unusual!* After only a day and a half in Rose's company, Annie already grew accustomed to the fact that wherever they go, people focus on Rose, treating Annie as if she were invisible.

*Do the Chantomes know who I am?*

Armand shoots a curious look at Annie. "I'd like you to meet my grandpa Jacques and my grandaunt Monique." He points to a middle-aged woman. "And my mom, Hélène, the beating heart of this place."

"My parents are the only ones who aren't part of the family business," Olivia remarks.

Rose looks up from her plate. "You're Monique's granddaughter, right?"

With a nod, Olivia sets her glass down and turns to Annie. "We've been speculating all afternoon, so I *have to* ask. Are you the Annie Malian from Granduncle René's postcard that I forwarded to Cassis about a week ago?"

Everybody freezes, their eyes on Annie.

"Yes," she says. "I am that Annie. How had you found me, by the way?"

"It was easy," Olivia replies. "You've kept your maiden name, and you're in the phone book."

Monique cups her wrinkled cheeks. "Goodness, I can't believe it! You really are the shy little maid from when we lived in Marseilles?"

Annie nods.

Monique and the others gasp delightedly. Jacques's aloof expression doesn't change.

Two waiters in Santa hats bring in the appetizer. It's a delicate sea bass tartare served on minimalist white plates.

Olivia had checked with Annie and Rose last night if the set menu for tonight worked for them. So, the food in itself isn't a surprise. What impresses Annie is how beautifully it's presented. You'd think it's a dish from a TV show!

The fish is finely diced; its texture and paleness contrast the crispness of the thinly sliced colorful tubers that frame it. A drizzle of yellowish-green olive oil adds a layer of richness. Greens, petals, and lemon quarters finish off this fine example of culinary prowess.

As Annie takes her first bite, the combination of the flavors explodes in her mouth. She closes her eyes in enjoyment. It's clear that the Chantomes were able to afford a gifted chef.

As she eats, she feels their eyes on her. Their curiosity is palpable. Annie glances at Rose who was supposed to be asking them questions but is too busy enjoying her food.

It's Monique who breaks the silence. "How have you been, Annie?"

"I stayed in Marseilles with my parents, after... the events. Found a job, got married, had two kids. I live in Cassis now with my oldest daughter and my son-in-law."

"Wonderful," Hélène cheers.

"When that postcard surfaced, you could've knocked me over with a feather," Monique says. "I had no idea you and René had been involved."

Annie shifts in her seat. "I'd asked him to keep our relationship secret."

"Were you afraid you'd lose your job?"

"Yes," Annie admits. "Your parents paid me well, and my family needed that income. Besides, we weren't getting married for the next few years, and I didn't want René to get into arguments with his mom and dad. You know how he was."

"Principled to the core," Monique says.

"A fraud," Jacques interjects.

Rose squints at him. "Why would you say that? Why would you call him a fraud?"

Unfortunately, it's Monique who answers before Jacques can explain himself, "René was the best of us. I'm sorry you had to suffer in silence when he took his life."

"Is that what you really think?" Annie levels her gaze with Monique's. "That your brother killed a man and then killed himself?"

A deafening silence engulfs the room.

*Why did I say that?! Did I ruin everything?* It was too direct, too soon. She should've let Rose do the talking, like they'd agreed.

"That's exactly what I think," Jacques says.

Monique turns to Hélène. "Do you mind relaying to your father that nobody cares about his opinion? Annie's question was for me."

"Will you tell your aunt," Jacques says to Hélène, "that I will express my opinions when I please? It's her problem they shatter her illusions, not mine."

The look of glum resignation on Hélène's face tells Annie

this has not been the first time Hélène's aunt and father have communicated through her.

"I have my doubts about suicide," Monique says to Annie. "As for the murder, I have never, not for a moment, believed that story. René killing his roommate out of jealousy? Preposterous!"

Olivia's eyes widen as if she's just realized something. "He'd written that sweet note to Annie when he was supposed to be in love with that other girl! That makes it even more implausible."

"Men do that sort of thing all the time," Jacques butts in.

Armand raises his hand, "I don't, Grandpa!"

"René wouldn't have either," Monique says.

Jacques sneers, "Oh, but I think he would. And I think he did."

Annie clenches her fists, fighting the temptation to throw her wine in his face. "No, he did not!"

*It wasn't enough to frame and kill your brother; you must soil his memory now?*

Monique turns to Hélène. "Can you please tell your dad that if he knows something about René that Annie and I don't, then perhaps, after all these years, he should share it with us?"

*Or confess to a double murder.*

Jacques's mouth twists as if he tastes something bad in his sea bass. He stares at Monique and then at Annie but says nothing.

The waiters clear the table and serve the main course of duck confit, its skin perfectly crisped, accompanied by dauphinoise potatoes.

"I'm going to go ahead and pop the question," Olivia says cheerfully, no doubt to lighten the mood. "Annie, is your visit a coincidence or was it triggered by the postcard?"

Glancing at Rose, Annie chooses her words with care. "I never believed the police version of the events... After I read the postcard, I knew that if there's one thing that I really want to do with the time I have left, it's to find out what really happened."

"Annie asked for my help in her quest." Rose hands out her business card.

*Rose Tassy*
*Queen of Beldoc*
*Doga Instructor*
*Amateur Detective (License to go pro pending)*

"Next year, I'll have my PI license," Rose says. "You know who to call if you need anything investigated."

Olivia studies the card. "So cool!"

"If you don't mind me asking," Rose says, "why did your family move to Le Crotoy?"

"My father went bankrupt shortly before René's death," Jacques replies. "He sold the business and the properties."

*That's weird...* "Before René's death?" Annie repeats. "But you still lived in the mansion. I worked there until after René died."

"The new owners weren't in a hurry," Jacques says. "They allowed us to stay on for a few months, until we found a new place. When we moved here, *Papa* invested what was left into this hotel."

"Les Tonneaux was in a terrible state when my grandparents bought it," Hélène chimes in.

"What had caused the bankruptcy?" Rose asks.

Jacques gives her a hard stare. "He never told us. All we knew was that one day our flourishing auction house sank like a brick."

"After René's death," Monique picks up, "*Maman* and *Papa* were keen to get out of Marseilles."

Rose nods. "That's understandable."

"The thing I never understood, though," Monique says, "is why resettle in Picardie, when Papa never even liked the North?"

Her gaze shifts from Rose to the business card next to her plate as if Rose's credentials meant she'd know the answer.

"Was your mother from the North?" Rose tries.

Monique shakes her head. "She was a born and raised Provençal, and she loved her region."

"They could've moved to Lyon," Rose muses. "It has more sunshine and opportunities in your late father's line of work than a village like Le Crotoy."

Monique gestures that she agrees. "They never told me why they did what they did, not knowing the first thing about the hotel business."

"And you?" Rose asks Jacques. "Did they tell you, by any chance?"

"No, but I suspected then, and I still do now, that it had to do with René's shady dealings."

"What do you mean, Papa?" Hélène asks.

His face tightens. "I can't tell you."

"Can't or won't?"

"Don't bother, my dear," Monique says to Hélène, waving dismissively. "What your father calls 'shady dealings' is simply René's political activism."

Even though Jacques doesn't confirm her statement, Annie can't see anything else it could be.

"He wanted to build a better world," she says with a dreamy smile.

"Oh, sweetie, he was doing a bit more than wanting!" Monique winks at her. "René was an active member of the PRAC, the Party of Radical Anti-Capitalists."

Annie stares at her. "I didn't know that."

"I didn't either," Monique reassures her. "But one day I

overheard Papa and René arguing about it. Papa wanted him to quit PRAC and focus on his studies."

Annie catches Rose's eye.

*Could PRAC be a lead, something worth looking into?*

Rose answers Annie's unspoken question with the tiniest of nods and then raises her glass. "To this reunion and to René's memory!"

"And to clearing his name!" Annie adds.

Everybody toasts to that except Jacques.

# CHAPTER 10

The first and shortest leg of the journey back to the South was over before it started. On the steam train, Annie and Rose talked nonstop. They replayed last night's dinner, recalling everything that had been said. They shared their impressions of the Chantome family and compared notes.

Rose agreed with Annie that René's older brother Jacques seemed suspicious. He made it clear he didn't hold René in high esteem. He tried to cast aspersions on his brother by hinting that he knew something about him that Monique and Annie didn't. Back when Annie worked in the Chantome house, Jacques was so neutral toward her that Annie never knew what to make of him. Now, she found him thoroughly unlikable.

Annie and Rose changed trains in Noyelles-sur-Mer. They're riding to Paris at present, and Rose is explaining to Annie that Jacques's rancor isn't proof of his guilt. It can't even be considered as evidence or a solid clue.

"Was Jacques away from Marseilles in the first days of January 1961?" Rose asks Annie.

"You mean if he could've been in Paris when René supposedly killed Grégoire and then himself?"

"I'm trying to figure out if he had an alibi," Rose says.

Annie rubs her chin. "I saw him around the house... He could've made day trips to Paris."

"It was a long journey back then," Rose adds.

"But not unfeasible."

While they wait for the high-speed train at the Gare de Lyon in Paris, they each place a phone call. Rose reaches out to her granddaughter Julie and asks if she or her sister Flo could gather information on the Party of Radical Anti-Capitalists that René had been a member of.

Annie calls her gendarme grandson Gabriel. She reports about her trip. Then she asks him to check if the gendarmerie or police databases has anything on PRAC that might be relevant.

Finally, the TGV to Marseilles arrives.

Just like on the trip from Marseilles to Paris, Annie and Rose have seats in different cars. Left alone with her thoughts, Annie dwells on the Chantomes' changing fortunes. They used to be one of Marseilles' wealthiest families. The patriarch, Pierre-François, was a very powerful man. If someone asked where she worked and she replied she was a maid in his house, they'd immediately treat Annie with more respect as if his stature rubbed off on her.

And then he lost his favorite son, the apple of his eye. Within months, his wealth and influence were gone, too. One of the reasons why the family moved so far away from Marseilles could be that it was hard for Pierre-François to cross familiar people. He saw pity in their eyes. Or schadenfreude. Or indifference where there used to be respect.

To their credit, Corinne and Pierre-François were able to pick themselves up and rebuild with the help of their remaining children. The Chantomes may not be as wealthy or influential as they were back in the day, but they're doing all right. More than all right.

The hotel is flourishing in Hélène's capable hands. As for the third generation, Olivia and Armand seem committed to the family business. Ah, if only Annie's own grandchildren had taken over Claire's shop! But, instead, each is pursuing his own career. Of the three, Gabriel's chosen path gives Annie the biggest headaches.

Today, being a gendarme is a risky, underpaid, and unappreciated occupation. They are the universal scapegoats. Politicians send them into the inferno without second thoughts—and then throw them under the bus. Annie would love Gabriel to get a different job. When his best friend quit after the Mob murdered his wife, Annie hoped Gabriel might follow suit. But his drive to serve proved stronger than his survival instinct.

Becoming a dad could change that. Unfortunately, the stubborn man has been breaking his mom's and granny's hearts by insisting he doesn't want kids.

As if on cue, he texts her.

> I'll meet you at the station. Can you confirm you received this text? Gabriel

After some fumbling, Annie manages to type a reply and send it off.

This isn't planned. She is supposed to take a cab at Marseille-Saint-Charles. But now she'll get to see Gabriel, the only one of her three grandsons who lives in a different town and who's often away on long and dangerous assignments.

Annie has no clue why he's coming to pick her up, but she won't waste her time guessing. It doesn't matter. Wins are so thin on the ground at her age that when life sends you one, you take it and you run.

~

WHEN ANNIE DISEMBARKS at the Marseille-Saint-Charles station, Rose is already waiting for her on the platform.

She grabs Annie's suitcase and rolls it alongside hers. "I had a message from Julie. She's meeting me here."

"I had a similar message from Gabriel," Annie says.

Exchanging an amused look, they start moving to the end of the platform. The rhythmic clatter of trains pulling in and out, the hum of conversations, and the occasional announcement combine into a familiar accompaniment. The air smells the same as it always does here, a mix of fuel, detergent, and perfumes spritzed with a faint salty tang of the Mediterranean Sea.

It's changed since Annie's youth with the varied kiosks, shops, and trendy eateries springing up. Oh, and the freaky artificial trees—pine cones grafted onto oak trunks—of the new hall.

The thing Annie has always loved about this station is the grand staircase leading up to it. Perched atop a hill, that station has a monumental cascade of stone steps. It used to make her feel like a conquering queen every time she descended it. Today, that small pleasure is yet another item on her ever-growing list of things she cannot do or would rather not do if she can help it.

"There, I can see them!" Rose points at something ahead.

Annie peers until she spots two familiar shapes. Julie and Gabriel wave and rush to them.

Gabriel gives Annie a hug. "I'm off today, so no excuse not to give my Medz Mama a lift."

She pats his cheek.

He points at Julie who's doing the southern quadruple cheek kiss routine with Rose. "Luckily, Julie was happy to tag along."

"My pâtisserie is closed on Sundays, so I had time on my hands," Julie says after greeting Annie.

"Are you driving with them to Cassis?" Rose asks her. "Or are you taking the local train to Beldoc with me?"

"I'll go back to Beldoc with you, Grandma."

Perhaps it's Julie's mention of the pâtisserie or the mouthwatering aroma of fresh pastries wafting from one of the station's bistros, but Annie is suddenly in no rush to get home.

"How about we sit down for a coffee and croissant before we leave Marseilles?" she asks.

Everybody approves of the idea. The young ones grab the suitcases, and the four of them make their way to the nearest café.

As soon as they're seated and served, Annie turns to Julie. "Did you know it was an Armenian man by the name of Harutyun who opened the first café in Marseilles?"

"I didn't," Julie says.

Rose asks, "When?"

"In the seventeenth century!"

Both Julie and Rose make impressed sounds.

Annie adds, "He then moved to London and opened the first coffeehouse there. And another Armenian opened the first café in Paris."

Gabriel touches her hand, a reproachful look in his chocolate eyes. "Medz Mama..."

*Does he* always *have to rain on my parade?*

Annie stares into the distance, pretending she didn't hear him and hoping someone will change the topic in the meantime. Unfortunately, no one intervenes to steer the conversation away from the quicksand.

"Come on, Annie," Gabriel says, urging her.

"Such a stickler for accuracy!" She blows her cheeks out, exasperated.

He nudges her. "So? Will you correct your earlier statement so that Julie and Rose don't unwittingly spread your fake news?"

"What I said about Marseilles is an established fact," Annie protests. "I might've exaggerated about London, which already had coffeehouses when Harutyun moved there."

Gabriel gives her hand a gentle squeeze. "I'm proud of you! It was a good start."

"What do you mean, a start?" She looks at him over the rims of her eyeglasses.

"The first café in Paris was opened by Procopio, an Italian man," he says to Rose and Julie. "The Armenian place did serve coffee, but it wasn't really a café."

"How do you know all that?" Rose asks.

He smiles. "Over the years, I've researched almost all of Annie's brags just so I could tell fact from fiction."

Annie tut-tuts, "You'd rather nitpick than let me glorify your ancestors. Why?"

"I'm a cop," he says, as if that explained everything.

*You have it backward, my boy!* You're a cop because you're a nitpicker.

"I did some research, too," Julie says, "after Rose called me."

Annie turns to her. *Couldn't you mention this a few minutes ago and spare me the unpleasantness?*

Aloud, she inquires, "Any luck?"

"I didn't have much time to dig, so what I found about the party René had joined, PRAC, is from today, not from 1961," she says apologetically.

"What did you find?" Rose asks.

"PRAC is being revived by Mikel Poupon, who's the grandson of the party's founder Etienne Poupon."

"Where are they based these days?" Annie asks.

"In Paris, just like the original edition."

Annie recoils at the thought of traveling to Paris to talk to this Mikel Poupon. *Honestly, why didn't he relaunch his party in the South?*

Julie pulls a small scratch pad from her purse and scans her notes. "Mikel has been quite successful with his relaunch, actually."

"How so?" Annie asks.

"The new PRAC started with just four members including Mikel Poupon and a woman with the last name Hugonet, same as Dany Hugonet who was the cofounder of the original PRAC. In less than two years, they grew to eight thousand members," Julie replies.

Rose gives her an incredulous stare. "That's a remarkable achievement!"

"I found recent articles and segments about them, so the movement is getting noticed by the media," Julie adds before closing the cover to her scratch pad. "That's all I have for now."

"I, too, found something after Annie called me," Gabriel says. "PRAC's old police file has been digitized in the meantime, so I could access it from my laptop."

Rose arches a surprised eyebrow. "PRAC had a file?"

"The police keep an eye on all political movements," he explains. "The ones that have *radical* in their name are practically begging to be monitored."

Everybody leans in, waiting for him to continue.

He wiggles his thick eyebrows. "Guess what? I found an interesting note from an intelligence officer in PRAC's file."

"What did it say?" Rose asks.

"That one of France's richest men at the time, Joel Gimbert, was secretly funding them."

Annie frowns. "Why would he do that?"

"Good question, considering that PRAC was a radical anti-capitalist party," Gabriel says.

"Maybe Joel Gimbert was an idealist, like René," Annie suggests. "Maybe he wanted to give all his money away."

"The Buddha did that!" Rose chimes in.

Gabriel leans back in his chair. "Except Joel Gimbert kept amassing more and more money and making himself and his family richer."

Rose shakes her head. "The Buddha didn't do that."

"Is Joel Gimbert still alive?" Annie asks.

"No, but his son, Blaise Gimbert is. Aaand... wait for it..." With a mischievous glint in his eyes, he looks from Annie to Rose to Julie.

"What?" the women ask simultaneously.

"Blaise Gimbert is funding PRAC's revival."

Annie slaps her thigh. "I say!"

Gabriel takes a moment to relish the effect of his statement on everybody's faces before adding, "Blaise has been as generous and as circumspect about his donations to PRAC as his father back in the day."

"Hang on, hang on!" Rose pinches the bridge of her nose. "In France, individual donations to parties are limited. I researched it back when I created mine to run for mayor of Beldoc."

"True, but nothing prevents every single adult in a family from making the maximum allowed contribution," Gabriel says. "If it's a large family, they add up."

"Are the Gimberts a large family?" Julie asks.

"Blaise has five siblings and six grown children," Gabriel replies. "All made maximum contributions. As did a bunch of his cousins, as well as his wife's parents and siblings. Thirty-one contributions in total."

"Big families are a politician's best friend." Julie giggles. "Better than a briefcase full of cash."

"Nothing is better than a briefcase full of cash," Rose declares before flicking a look at Gabriel. "Where does Blaise Gimbert live these days?"

"In Monaco, mostly."

A smile curves Rose's lips as she turns to Annie, "We can drive there on Tuesday. It's a day trip."

"Rose, Medz Mama," Gabriel casts them a warning look. "I do not recommend stalking a man like Blaise Gimbert."

Rose pats his hand. "Darling, who said anything about stalking? I have a much better idea."

# CHAPTER 11

ose received some disturbing news when she got home from Le Crotoy yesterday afternoon, and she's been restless ever since. This morning, as she walked Lady and did her grocery shopping, she could barely concentrate.

Now she sits at her computer, trying to study for her upcoming exams, but all she can think is: *Why would he do that?*

Her ex-boyfriend, widowed notary Serge Guichard, volunteered to be one of Beldoc's Santas this year. That means he'll be going to the European Santa Convention in Paris. Last year, Serge had paid off Rose's huge credit card debt, saving her house from foreclosure. She was infinitely grateful, but she broke up with him. Not because she'd stopped caring about him—she still does—but she couldn't be with a man to whom she owed a large sum of money. They would no longer be equals in their relationship. She'd feel cheapened like a kept woman.

Her plan was for them to remain friends while she would

look for a way to pay him back. As soon as she'd repaid him, they could reunite as a couple.

But Serge didn't go with her plan. He refused to be a friend of Rose's. Deeply hurt that she'd expect him to treat her differently just because he'd lent her money, he told her he wanted all or nothing.

She chose nothing.

He cut her off.

A few months later, he started dating another woman. And now he'll be going to Paris with the small delegation from Beldoc consisting of Rose, the newsdealer Adonis who's the town's usual Santa, and the mayor's secretary Chantal who will be doing the hand-holding. Chantal told Rose that Serge would be bringing his girlfriend along at his expense.

*Why? Why would he do that to me?*

To distract herself from the distress, Rose calls Annie. "Hope I didn't wake you up?"

"I was about to take a nap, but we can talk."

"What do you think of Gabriel's intel regarding the Gimberts?"

Annie takes a moment before replying, "Jacques is still my prime suspect. But if a megarich capitalist is caught funding the sworn enemies of capitalism, I suppose he should expect pushback from his peers."

"I imagine he'd be considered a traitor to his class," Rose says. "He wouldn't want such a stain on his image, would he?"

"Clearly not, because he wouldn't want his donations to PRAC known."

Rose's thoughts jump straight to René. "What if... What if René found out and asked Joel to clarify his motives?"

"You mean confirm that his funding didn't come with strings attached?" Annie says with a chuckle.

"Something like that." Rose scratches the back of her

head. "Say, René concluded that Joel's was trying to corrupt PRAC. What would he have done?"

"He might've decided to expose Joel for the snake that he was."

A bulb goes off in Rose's head. "And to stop him, Joel might've acted preemptively by eliminating René!"

"Um... Sounds weak as a motive."

"Your theory about Jacques is weaker than that, if you ask me."

After a brief silence, Annie asks, "What did you mean yesterday when you said you had a way to approach Joel's son?"

"A close friend of mine is the editor in chief of our local paper, *Beldoc Live.* I'll ask her to get one of her reporters to request an interview with Blaise Gimbert."

"Assuming she okays it, why would Blaise Gimbert agree to be interviewed on such a thorny subject?" Annie asks.

"Precisely because it's thorny! Blaise would want to control the narrative."

Annie harrumphs. "Call me if you manage to set up an interview."

"A little gratitude, maybe?" Rose puffs, annoyed. "I'm doing this for free in case you forgot."

"I'm sorry," Annie says after a brief silence. "You're trying hard, Rose, and I'm being unappreciative... and unhelpful. It won't do."

Surprised by her sincere apology, Rose mutters "Talk soon" and hangs up.

Rose, in her Hollywood sunglasses and silk scarf, is at the wheel of a rented Alfa Romeo, which she managed to get in a yellow hue just as bright as her Nissan's. Next to her in the passenger seat is *Beldoc Live's* star reporter Noam Toche. In the back, Annie is sharing the space with Lady. In an unfortunate pileup of coincidences, everyone from Sarah to Julie to Flo to Karl was unavailable to feed and walk Lady this afternoon. And so, Rose had no other choice but to take her with them to Monaco.

Officially, she splurged one hundred euros for eight hours in this car because her two-seater couldn't fit the four of them. But, of course, it's obvious that she could've rented a much cheaper four-seater. Fortunately for Rose, both Annie and Noam have so far been polite enough not to point that out. They probably told themselves it was her money, after all— she could spend it any way she pleased.

The thing is Rose's previous visit to Monaco had been a very chic affair. Serge took her there on a weekend. They stayed in a five-star hotel in Monte Carlo, dined like royals, dressed like celebrities, and gambled at the casino all night.

Rose simply couldn't return there on a shoestring now. Even if her ex wouldn't see it, she wanted her post-Serge visit to Monaco to be comme il faut. For that, she needed a befitting car, and this sleek Italian thing was just the ticket.

Her mistake was to skip the built-in GPS in a bid to save a few euros. She'd planned to use the app on her phone. But said app went on strike the moment they set off. It keeps freezing up and won't talk to her. As a result, Rose is forced to pay attention to road signs and rely on her passengers' map-reading skills. *Back to the Middle Ages!*

"Two hours each way," Noam tut-tuts next to her. "I had better things to do with my day."

He's been like this since the beginning of the trip. Marie-Jo ordered him to accompany Rose and Annie to Monaco, and he isn't thrilled, and he's making sure Rose knows it. It annoys him that he, Noam Toche, Beldoc's best investigative reporter, must spend a full workday indulging his boss's cronies.

"I mean it, why couldn't you interview Blaise Gimbert on your own?" he asks, pestering Rose. "You manage just fine when you help Julie and her gang with their cases."

"We do ask for your help sometimes," Rose reminds him. "Like, last year when you interviewed the pharma boss, Paul Sivry. Remember?"

"How could I forget?"

"It's a similar situation," Rose says. "Blaise Gimbert agreed to do the interview because the request came from a legit newspaper. Besides, I'm sure his security will check your press card."

Noam twists his mouth, "I'm a journalist, not a figurehead with a press card!"

"And you'll get to *journalize* to your heart's content after Annie and I have asked *our* questions."

From the back seat, Annie says placatingly, "I'm sure it'll turn out to be an exciting interview for all of us, Monsieur Toche."

He ignores her effort, addressing Rose again, "I just want to know how you managed to persuade Marie-Jo to send me on this assignment. What did you offer in exchange?"

"To chronicle our delegation's time at the Santa Convention in Paris with photos and juicy gossip," Rose replies. "One of your colleagues will make entertaining posts out of it and write a feature."

Noam grumbles, "Great. Beldoc's only serious reporter is indentured in exchange for a bit of gossip from the Santa Convention. The ignominy!"

"Stop bickering and enjoy the scenery," Annie urges them from the back seat.

Rose looks to her right. They are now driving along an inland highway between Cannes and Antibes. From time to time, the Mediterranean Sea peeks out in the distance, sparkling under the December sun. Rose recalls that when she went to Monaco with Serge, he covered this stretch on a much more scenic route. She decides she can find it and veers off the main road.

"What are you doing?" Noam squeaks.

She infuses her voice with confidence. "Trust me."

"To do what?"

"To take you to a hidden gem." She turns onto an even narrower road, glancing in the rearview mirror. "Prepare for some of the best views of Riviera!"

A few minutes later, the road morphs into a dirt path zigzagging between farms.

"Are you sure this is the right way?" Noam asks.

Rose waves him off, her eyes on the road.

Soon, the remaining houses give way to open fields. There is still no expanse of water in sight. Rose's confidence wavers.

"This doesn't seem right," she murmurs, scanning the rural landscape.

Before she knows it, they're in the middle of a farmer's field, next to a fluffy white flock.

Noam stares out the window. "What the what? We're being surrounded by sheep!"

"Nah, they're clouds," Annie claims. "Miniature, ground-level, bleating clouds."

Annie and Rose burst into laughter.

"Ha. Ha. Hilarious," Noam says.

Lady becomes alert and presses her nose against the glass. Her floppy ears perk up as much as they can at the sight of the wooly creatures. She wags her tail slow and low, which translates as, "I'm watching you. Don't you dare try anything funny!"

One particularly curious ewe ambles over to the car and glues its nose against Lady's, separated by the pane of glass. Lady draws back, her tail wagging harder. She bares her teeth and growls aggressively.

The sight of her small, pampered dog threatening the much larger sheep fills Rose with pride. *You go, girl!* Squaring her shoulders, Rose attempts to maneuver the car around the sheep. It takes time, but the flock ends up parting to let them pass, and Rose manages to navigate the vehicle out of the field.

As they hit the dirt path, leaving the sheep behind, Noam turns to Rose. "That was the most scenic route I've ever taken." His voice laced with sarcasm, he adds, "A gem, indeed!"

"Wasn't it?" she deadpans. "I bet you'll never forget that view."

Rose's navigation app chooses that moment to awaken from its coma and talk to her. Ten minutes later, they're back on the highway, speeding toward Monaco again.

# CHAPTER 12

From her seat, Annie watches Rose maneuver the Alfa Romeo into the underground garage. The car lurches into a parking spot after a few near misses and narrowly avoids a scrape against the concrete wall. A string of colorful curses escapes Rose's lips, sapping the image of gentility she's keen to project.

"*Bordel de merde!*" Rose grumbles. "I'm not used to four-seaters anymore."

Noam opens the door on his side. "This trip is turning out to be more eventful than I expected. First the wilderness and the sheep, now the freestyle parking..." He rolls his eyes. "I can feel the adrenaline surging in my veins."

Rose gets out and opens Annie's door.

Annie hands the dog to her before calling to Noam, "Can you give me a hand, please?"

He rushes toward her. With Noam's help, she climbs out of the car on wobbly legs. They surface from underground in La Condamine, Monaco's business quarter. Rose takes Lady to a nearby grassy area. Her tail high, the furball pads around, sniffing the grass. Once she's picked her spot, she goes to potty, looking up at Rose with an air of proud achievement that only dogs can have in this circumstance.

Rose coos, "That's it, *ma chérie*. Good girl!"

When Lady is done, Rose cleans up after her, and then the four of them head toward the snazzy office building where they are scheduled to meet with Blaise Gimbert. The elevator ride to the top floor is too short to admire the cityscape unfolding outside its glass walls. Annie marvels at the view— the blend of classic and ultramodern, the glittering sea, the rocking yachts in Port Hercule... Annie has been to Monaco several times, but the grandeur of this tiny city-state that the locals call The Rock and the amount of wealth per square meter will never cease to baffle her.

A secretary leads them to Blaise Gimbert's corner office. A security guard at the entrance checks Noam's press card. When he asks to see Rose's and Annie's cards, Noam tells him they are freelancers, a photographer and a fact-checker, working with *Beldoc Live*. The guard inspects their IDs.

"Can we go in now?" Noam asks.

The security guard cracks his knuckles. "In a moment."

He pats them down and takes their phones, leaving Noam's professional recorder and Rose's camera.

The guard points at the dog. "What's his role?"

"Hers," Rose corrects him. "Lady is my emotional support animal. She is vital to my work, and she is very well-behaved."

He gives Rose a sardonic, heavy-lidded look but lets them in.

Everything about the vast office speaks to Blaise's status and power. With no curtains or blinds to impede it, sunlight streams over the polished wood floors and leather sofas. The floor-to-ceiling windows offer a breathtaking view of the city and the harbor. The office is eerily silent. Even with all the hustle and bustle of the city below, not a single sound, not even the faintest whisper, pierce these walls of glass and steel.

Blaise, a trim man in his sixties looks up from a document on his desk. "Please, have a seat."

As they settle into the designer chairs, Noam turns on his recorder. Rose takes a few photos of Blaise, while Noam gives him their agreed-upon spiel. He is preparing an investigative piece for *Beldoc Live* on the successful revival of PRAC by Mikel Poupon. The article would be incomplete without interviewing Blaise Gimbert, the discreet sponsor of said revival.

If Blaise is surprised to hear that the cat is out of the bag, he doesn't show it.

Instead, he inclines his head to one side and asks Noam, "Why is the local press in Provence interested in the revival of PRAC?"

While Noam scrambles for a plausible reason, Annie answers the question, "Because a Provence man, René Chantome, who died under tragic circumstances many years ago, had been active in the original PRAC. The article will feature both René and the party."

Blaise's face is still as unreadable as before.

"So," Noam picks up, "tell me, why sponsor Mikel Poupon's revived PRAC?"

"Because elections are coming up," Blaise says. "A nice lineup of European, national, regional, and municipal elections, all happening over the next two years. The timing is perfect."

"That's the tactical side of it," Rose says. "But what's the strategy here? Why fund a radical anti-capitalist party whose goals are against your self-interest as a tycoon?"

"Wouldn't it make more sense for you to sponsor a right-wing party?" Noam asks.

"I can't help it." Blaise sneers. "It's my self-destructive streak."

Noam folds his arms over his chest as if to show he won't let Blaise get away with a joke.

Blaise tries again. "What? You don't believe me? I'll have you know that self-sabotage is a very common disorder."

"I'm sure it is." Rose sweeps her hand around the opulent office. "But such a disorder would've made your level of success unattainable."

Noam nods. "The ultrarich tend to be highly rational. They tend to put their self-interest above all else. It's how they become in the first place and stay rich."

"We know that your father, Joel, funded the original PRAC in 1960," Annie says, eager to stay on topic. "What was his goal?"

"You really want to know?" Blaise asks her.

Everybody nods.

He points at the recorder. "Turn it off. I'm willing to satisfy your curiosity, but only off the record. You will keep it out of your article."

"All right." Noam switches the recorder off.

"My father loved chess, and he made sure I learned to play it well," Blaise begins. "The Gimbert family's support for PRAC is, to use the modern jargon, 4D chess."

Annie meets his gaze. "Some of us are eighty-four. Can you explain what you mean, please?"

"I will," he says, "just like I did to the reporter before you, who also thought she was onto the scoop of the century."

"I don't think this is the scoop of the century," Noam interjects.

Annie peers at Blaise. "Who's the other reporter? Who else has uncovered this information?"

Blaise waves her off. "It doesn't matter. What matters is the big picture. Funding a party like PRAC may appear counterproductive for someone in my position, but it is a rational choice."

"How is it rational?" Rose asks. "The anti-capitalists hate the rich, don't they?"

"Yet they happily take our money."

Noam shrugs. "They think they're using you, and you think you're using them. The question is, who's astute and who's deluded?"

"My father's net worth was two hundred million when he died," Blaise says. "I'm worth two billion. And I pay less tax than he did."

"Looks like the Gimberts are the astute ones," Rose offers. "You're the ones using PRAC, and they're the ones getting used."

Blaise wags his forefinger. "Not so fast!"

"What do you mean?" she asks with a frown.

"What if they don't mind being used by us?" He lifts an eyebrow. "What if our arrangement is mutually beneficial? They get to be the noble champions of the poor at no personal cost. They get the good image and the perks without spending a dime of their own money."

Rose widens her eyes theatrically. "Oh no! Are you insinuating the politicians lie to the public about their goals?"

"I'm not insinuating," Blaise says with a crooked smile.

Noam rubs his chin. "So, basically your family and PRAC are in a symbiotic relationship."

"That's one way to describe it," Blaise says. "Mind you, it's a tacit understanding between us. Nothing on paper. My father was obsessed with keeping our financial support for PRAC secret."

Annie gives him a slit-eyed look. "Not you?"

"To me, it isn't such a big deal. In fact, my shrewdest friends advertise their support for revolutionary movements."

"Don't your friends face backlash from their peers?" Rose asks. "Don't journalists scream 'hypocrite' at them?"

Blaise chuckles softly. "My friends own and keep afloat all the mainstream media across the political spectrum." He turns to Annie. "That's what I mean by 4D chess, madame."

"I understand now, thank you." Annie feels her blood pressure rise from the frustration of getting nowhere. "Tell me something, how far would your father have gone to keep his secret?"

Blaise's smile fades away.

"Say, someone had found out about the funding," Annie plows on. "Not a reporter, but an idealistic PRAC member. Would your father have sent a hitman to end him?"

Blaise glares at her. "Never!"

"The political climate was different in the sixties, Monsieur Gimbert," Annie says. "Protecting his secret might've been important enough for your father to resort to extreme measures."

"Like ordering a hit job?" Blaise snorts with derision. "Preposterous!"

"How can you be so sure?" Rose asks.

Blaise reaches for something under his desk while pointing his chin at the door. "Mesdames, monsieur, we're done here. Goodbye."

The security guard opens the door from the other side and snarls at Annie's group, "This way."

Noam, Rose, and Annie rise from their seats. Rose picks up Lady and holds her to her chest, either out of protectiveness or for emotional support like she'd claimed. Annie doesn't know her well enough yet to decide which.

Before they leave his office, Blaise points a finger at Noam. "You do not have my permission to print anything that was said here today. I will sue your paper out of existence if you disregard my wish."

"Rest easy," Noam says. "*Beldoc Live's* owner is one of your 'shrewd friends.'"

Shakespeare comes to mind as Annie follows Noam and Rose out the door.

*All the world's a stage,*
   *And all the men and women merely players.*

# CHAPTER 13

*R*ose carefully folds her *Arlésienne* costume to put it in her suitcase for Paris. She'll wear it at the European Santa Convention the day after tomorrow. After she's done packing, she'll deliver Lady to Sarah's. Then she'll meet the rest of the Beldoc delegation in front of the town hall. A minibus will take them to Arles, where they'll catch the TGV to Paris.

*To think that only a week ago I was thrilled about this trip!*

Rose was going to have so much fun at Santa Con! Her granddaughter Cat, who lives in Paris and whom Rose doesn't see nearly enough, was going to attend the Queens of Provence side event, and then have lunch with Rose. In the afternoon, Rose was going to have a blast with Adonis and Chantal, and in the evening, all three were going to go to the banquet organized by the European Association of Santas and Father Christmases.

Rose is still looking forward to those things, but she dreads watching Serge shower his new girlfriend with signs of affection that used to be for her.

To distract herself from those thoughts while she packs, Rose replays yesterday's interview with Blaise Gimbert in her mind. It didn't go well. Everybody sulked on the way back, which made the return trip feel longer than the off-piste drive to Monaco, sheep and all.

Later that evening Rose had called Annie to discuss where they stood with the investigation. The conclusion was... on a cul-de-sac.

Annie's late husband Andre Bogossian, who was Rose's first suspect, had a damn solid alibi. They put René's brother Jacques and Blaise's father Joel on the back burner until something tangible surfaced that implicated them.

The original leadership of PRAC, Etienne Poupon and Dany Hugonet had died a natural death—Etienne a decade ago, and Dany earlier this year. Bernadette, the supposed bone of contention between René and his roommate Grégoire, passed away five years back.

The only person from that group that could still be alive was Bernadette's best friend Marie. Annie met her once when she visited René in Paris. But assuming Marie was still alive, how does one find someone without a photo, a last name, or an address?

Still, it was a shame not to profit from Rose's upcoming stay in Paris. And so, it was decided that she'd try to talk to Etienne Poupon's grandson Mikel, the one who's relaunching PRAC. Neither Rose nor Annie expects anything useful to come out of that interview, but it's the only lead they have at the moment.

It's also the only reason Rose hasn't canceled her participation in Santa Con. Two train trips and an entire day in the company of her ex and his new girlfriend terrify Rose, for sure. But the risk of failing the first ever case she investigates as the lead detective scares her even more. After all, it is her and not Julie or Flo who envisions a career as a licensed PI. If she can't resolve Annie's cold case, Rose fears she'll start doubting she has what it takes to be a private detective.

She should've never taken it on! But now that she has, she'll be damned if she doesn't give it all she's got.

~

ON THE HIGH-SPEED train from Arles to Paris, Rose is lucky enough to have a window seat across the aisle from the others. She stares at the countryside blurring past in a wash of muted winter hues. It won't be possible to avoid socializing with the rest of her group for very long, but that's all right. It isn't her goal. Her goal is to have as little contact as possible with Serge.

*Did he really have to be so dashing today in his fine wool suit and bow tie?*

His new girlfriend, on the other hand, looks like a smudge. Rose has been keeping Josephine out of her line of sight so successfully that the woman's body shape and facial features are still a mystery to her.

Fortunately, Rose gets along well with her other two fellow travelers. She's known and liked newsdealer Adonis Khoury for at least thirty years. And, even though Victor's secretary Chantal isn't exactly a friend of Rose's, they share a certain pragmatism that has saved many a municipal council meeting from ending in fisticuffs. Chantal loves Paris, its shops and its Christmas lights, so she persuaded Victor to send her to Santa Con as the group coordinator. To make sure her role is clear to everyone, she always has a manila folder and a phone in her hands.

That reminds Rose that she could use the long trip to do some research for her case, like a professional PI would. Shifting her eyes from the window, she googles the Party of

Radical Anti-Capitalists on her phone. Their official website presents PRAC's vision and its new face, Mikel Poupon. She learns that it's been Mikel's dream since kindergarten to resuscitate his grandfather's legacy.

Together, Mikel Poupon and his comrades will succeed where their predecessors failed. They will take PRAC all the way to the presidential office.

Rose checks the other sections of the website. Unsurprisingly, Gimbert isn't mentioned anywhere, not even on the "Donate Now" page. At the top of that page, there's a box featuring a fundraising party tomorrow evening at the cultural center at 104 rue d'Aubervilliers. The tickets aren't cheap.

Rose hesitates. If she goes to the event, she can approach Mikel in an uncontrived way and ask him a few questions about his grandpa. Perhaps more importantly, attending the PRAC fundraiser would give her an excuse to skip the banquet tomorrow, where Serge and Josephine will no doubt be present.

Finally, the fete promises a great DJ and a lot of dancing, which Rose adores.

She buys an e-ticket straight from the website, marveling at how technically advanced it is. In comparison, she had no website at all when she ran for mayor of Beldoc. Her granddaughter Flo put her on social media and made a few posts for her during the campaign. Clothilde had some flyers printed, which Sarah, Julie and Eric handed out. But that was it.

Chantal's commanding voice rises over the hum of the train, interrupting Rose's comparative analysis. "Everybody to the bar car!"

"Good idea." Adonis jumps to his feet. "I'm hungry."

Serge and Josephine stand up.

Chantal turns to Rose. "Come on, I must brief you all."

"Must you?" Rose asks resignedly.

She knows Chantal too well to put up any serious resistance. She picks up her purse and follows the others to the bar car. When they get there, Chantal herds her charges to a vacant corner by the window and takes their orders.

"My treat!" Serge, ever the gentleman, announces. "I insist."

"That's kind of you, but the budget Victor allocated to us covers this," Chantal says.

Josephine claps her hands. "We're so lucky! We have the best mayor in Provence!"

*Is she doing this on purpose? Does she know I ran against him?*

Rose still won't look at her.

Adonis jumps in after Chantal. "I'll help you."

*Nooooo! Don't leave me alone with Serge and Josephine!*

But it's too late. Chantal and Adonis are already at the end of the line snaking around the counter.

Josephine turns toward Rose. "Serge and I have been trying to figure out what makes a really good Santa. He's keen to get it right."

"Uh-huh," Rose says, her gaze fixed on the passing scenery outside the window.

"A hearty laugh is essential, right?" Josephine carries on. "Ho ho ho!"

Rose doesn't deign to react.

Serge levels his eyes with hers. "Come on, Rose, you're a sensible person—"

"How dare you insult me like that?"

He recoils from her withering look. "I apologize. You aren't a sensible person. In fact, you're the antithesis of such a person."

Josephine's gaze shifts from him to Rose. "Is there a

history here I'm not privy to? Have you guys had a falling out over something?"

"You're new in town, aren't you?" Rose asks her with the briefest of glances.

Josephine looks sweet enough. And a decade younger than Rose.

*I hate her.*

"I moved in nine months ago, as soon as I retired," Josephine says.

"From where?"

"Rouen."

Rose rolls her shoulders back. "Provence isn't for everyone."

"She survived the mosquitoes in summer and the mistral in the fall," Serge says. "She'll do fine."

Josephine addresses Rose, "I find it so progressive that Beldoc elected you to be its queen!"

*Because I'm too old for that?*

Rose trains her eyes on Serge. *Is she being mean or just obtuse?*

He shifts from one foot to the other.

An awkward silence settles between the three of them. Josephine's expectant gaze remains on Rose. Serge studies his hands. Rose stares out the window, listening to the murmur of wrappers, punctuated by the ping of the microwave timer.

"Hey, Jo, did you know Rose is a doga instructor?" Serge tries.

Rose glares at him. "Let's leave the dogs out of it, shall we?"

Serge raises his hands as if to signal he's giving up and leans back in his seat. Fortunately, Chantal and Adonis arrive with the orders. Chantal launches into a host of practical details concerning the hotel, the venue, and the location of the restaurant for the banquet afterward.

"It's a shame I won't be able to attend the banquet," Rose declares.

Chantal stares at her. "Why not?"

Rose flashes the e-ticket on her phone at the bewildered Chantal. "Because saving France from capitalism is well worth a dinner. *Vive la République!*"

# CHAPTER 14

*T*he morning side event, Queens of Provence, was a great success. From Rose's perspective, at any rate. Cat arrived early, and they chatted by the coffee machine during a disappointingly dull public lecture, "Queen, Santon, Santa: Exploring the Unexpected Connections between Traditions."

After the lecture was over, Rose fulfilled her duties as Queen of Beldoc. The experience wasn't the least bit tedious. What with Rose being the oldest among the queens by a long shot, she quickly became the center of attention. The organizers were eager to show her off. The reporters scrambled to interview her. The public asked for autographs and took selfies.

At the end of the event, the participants received certificates and goodie bags. Most of the other queens left at that point. Rose had a lovely meal with Cat. A professional medium, Cat shared recent anecdotes from her work and finally showed Rose pictures of her boyfriend Zack whom Rose has yet to meet.

After lunch, Cat went back to her office.

Rose wandered around the huge trade fair center for twenty minutes until she found hall 1. Decorated with bright garlands, mistletoe and lights, Santa Con's main program is still underway since this morning.

Rose makes heads turn as she picks her way through the hall. She's dressed in her traditional Provençal costume complete with a fitted bodice, layered skirt, fine shawl, and a fan. A miniature white lace bonnet known as the fichu is wrapped around the chignon on the top of her head. Her neckline is cut low and her Wonderbra gives a youthful pertness to her breasts.

That being said, Rose is aware that Wonderbra-enhanced cleavage shouldn't take all the credit for the attention. Any woman who looks as if she stepped straight out of the sun-drenched pages of a Marcel Pagnol book would stand out in a room full of men dressed for the North Pole.

She opens her embroidered reticule, pulls out a smartphone and texts Chantal.

> Where are you?

Waiting for the reply, she surveys the sea of red and white around her. Hundreds of bearded Santas and Father Christmases chatter in French, English, and other tongues as they mill about in groups. Festive tunes drift from the speakers, serving as a lo-fi background to the jingling bells, laughter, children's cheers, and caroling that resound throughout the hall.

Christmassy scents fill the air—pine, spiced cookies, hot cocoa, orange...

Chantal replies to Rose's text.

> Look to your left.

Peering in the recommended direction, Rose spots

Chantal waving at her and hurries in her direction. Then she sees the others. Adonis, a seasoned Santa, is in his element. With his hands resting on his protruding belly, which is real—unlike his white beard—he's giving tips to a cluster of wide-eyed newbies.

"Remember, kids can smell lack of conviction," he teaches them. "When asked if you're a real Santa, you don't hesitate. You say, 'Of course, I am.' Because you are!"

His disciples nod.

"And never, ever make promises without checking with the parents first," Adonis continues. "If the kid asks for a puppy, there's no way you say yes unless you know it's in the pipeline. A child's trust is a precious gift, and we Santas must never break it!"

Chantal is talking with a vendor.

With the enthusiasm of a first-timer, Serge is trying on a pair of tall Santa boots. They must be too big for him because his attempts to walk straight result in a series of near falls.

"Sweetie, you're hilarious!" Josephine giggles, her camera out to capture every moment.

He grins at her. "To be a Santa isn't just to embrace the spirit of Christmas. It's also to celebrate the ridicule!"

*Oh, dear. He has really moved on, hasn't he?*

Until this moment, Rose had been convinced that Serge's new relationship was his way to make her regret breaking up with him. But now, watching them interact, she isn't so sure anymore.

*They look happy together.*

She turns away before either of them can notice her discomfiture and rushes to the nearest vendor's stand. It displays a cornucopia of gadgets and gizmos under the sign Safety First for Santas, Reindeers, and Elves.

The vendor, a jovial man with a twinkle in his eye, gives

her his sales pitch, "I have selected every single item you see here with the safety of Santas and their helpers in mind."

He goes on to demo a Santa suit with extra-sturdy padding, perfect for those tricky chimney descents.

"The padding also protects against small-to-medium-sized knives," he comments. "A useful feature these days for Santas that are out after dark."

Rose surveys his fare. A display of whistles and personal alarms shaped like little Christmas bells reminds her of Julie's and Cat's investigation in Paris two years ago. An alarm like this—of a classic non-Santa variety—saved the twins' lives. Rose got one for herself at the time. But the device went off inside her purse during a dinner at a fine restaurant, so she got rid of it.

Behind the alarms, there's a stack of fluorescent yellow vests in two sizes, elf and Santa. Reflective harnesses are available for reindeer in one size.

The vendor follows her gaze. "They ensure that a real or pantomime reindeer will be seen even on the foggiest of Christmas Eves."

Also in two sizes, he sells Santa and elf hats with special lining.

"They're called EMF hats, because they act like a Faraday cage around your head," the vendor explains. "In case electromagnetic waves are a concern."

Pepper sprays disguised as candy canes hang from hooks on a string. Their harmless appearance is quite a contrast to their contents. If it weren't for the sign, Rose would've never guessed what they were.

Rose points at them. "Aren't these illegal?"

"In some countries, yes," the vendor says. "But in France, you're allowed to carry a spray can under one hundred milliliters, if you have a legitimate reason to do so."

"Who decides if my reason is legitimate?"

"The cop who might find it on you." He winks. "If you're in the habit of showing that much cleavage, any cop would agree you have a legitimate reason to carry a pepper spray."

"The low cut is part of my Arlésienne costume, you ignorant man!" It strikes Rose that in her youth, she'd be out after midnight in a low-cut micro dress, and feel perfectly safe. She'd go topless on the beach and feel safe, too.

*What changed?* What happened to men in the intervening years? Why do women need to cover themselves more today than they did fifty years ago? What's the end point to this trend?

"I'll take the pepper spray," she says.

As the day progresses, Rose sticks with Adonis and Chantal while avoiding Serge and Josephine. She tries on several Santa hats, takes a selfie with a reindeer prop, and gets into a heated debate with an elf about real versus artificial Christmas trees.

Toward the end of the afternoon, she ends up among the public watching the Ho Ho Ho Contest. Each participant gives it his all. An elderly Santa, his cheeks flushed with effort, bellows out a ho ho ho so forceful that his false teeth fly out. Everybody gasps when the partial denture lands in Rose's cleavage. A few half-suppressed giggles break out around her.

She plucks the teeth out with the tip of her shawl and hands back to the Santa. "You might need these for the banquet."

The public hoots.

His eyes on Rose's décolleté, the Santa inserts the teeth and winks at her. "My teeth just had a taste of heaven, madame. Do you really think they care for a banquet?"

His cheeky come-on leaves Rose speechless.

"May I sit next to you tonight?" he asks.

"No, you may not," she says archly. "And I won't be there, anyway."

She blows a kiss to Chantal and Adonis, turns on her heel, and heads to the cloakroom.

# CHAPTER 15

*I*n her hotel room Rose swaps her flamboyant Arlésienne costume for a pair of blue jeans, a white shirt, a black leather motorcycle jacket, and a coat to protect her from the cold outside. She applies some makeup and transfers the contents of her reticule to her regular purse. She sticks the candy cane spray in there, too.

In addition to saving the French Republic from evil capitalists, Rose has several goals for tonight. She plans to dance. She intends to meet Mikel Poupon, the grandson of the founder of PRAC, and see what he knows. Striking up casual conversations with the guests and listening in on their tittle-tattle is also on her program. While it's unlikely that anyone at that fete will gossip about a cold case from 1961, they might mention something useful.

And even if it isn't, gossip is fun.

The *métro* and a short walk get her to the cultural center in the 19th arrondissement. Inside the vast building, Rose quickly finds the right room. It's already abuzz with activity, decorated in the spirit of a nostalgic nod to *bals populaires*

—the festive public dance events born after the French Revolution and immortalized by Renoir.

Strings of colorful lights crisscross the ceiling. The scent of fresh bread and cheese wafts from a corner, mingling with the aroma of liquors and strong coffee. A makeshift dance floor occupies the center. Three couples are performing *le roc*, a genteel boogie-woogie. Off to the side, two volunteers behind a table sell raffle tickets.

Rose beelines to the table.

"You already did your part by purchasing an entry ticket for this fete," one of them says to her. "But if you buy one or more raffle tickets, you'll help PRAC even more!"

The tickets are inexpensive, so Rose gets ten.

A handsome man in his mid-thirties spots her from across the room. He makes his way over, accompanied by a woman pushing forty.

"Bonsoir," he greets Rose. "Thank you for supporting PRAC! My name is Mikel Poupon. My wife Katia and I are hosting this fundraising fete."

"I'm Rose Tassy, a retired teacher from Provence, as you can probably guess from my accent," Rose introduces herself. "Please, call me Rose."

Half listening to the string of niceties from Katia about the central role teachers play in the republic, Rose ogles Mikel. He has a winsome smile, black hair and striking eyes—one green, the other blue. He isn't merely handsome, she realizes. He's downright gorgeous.

"You've done a great job, Mikel and Katia," she says. "Amazing ambiance!"

Mikel laughs. "We certainly hope so."

"We want everyone to have fun tonight, as a thank-you for their support," Katia chimes in.

Cocking his head, Mikel studies Rose. "If I may, what moved you to sponsor the Party of Radical Anti-Capitalists through this fundraiser and the raffle? I saw you bought ten tickets."

"I've always been a radical," Rose says.

*Just not like you think.*

"Fantastic!" Mikel rubs his hands together. "Would you consider becoming a card-carrying member of PRAC?"

"I'd love to, but I'm already a founding member of another party."

Katia hikes an intrigued eyebrow. "Which?"

"We're called Elf, which stands for 'Environment, Life, Future'," Rose says. "I launched it two years ago, when I ran for mayor of my town."

"What's Elf's current membership?" Mikel asks.

"Um... Eleven and a half."

"That's remarkable, Rose! Eleven thousand five hundred members for such a recent party is quite an achievement," Katia enthuses.

Mikel smiles his winsome smile. "And here I was thinking PRAC was in a league of its own!"

Tempting as it is, Rose can't let such a glaring misunderstanding go unchecked.

"ELF has eleven people and a dog with no voting rights," she says.

Mikel gapes. "Ah."

The Poupons exchange an amused look and move on to greet someone else.

Trying not to think about the four-course menu at Santa Con banquet, Rose heads to the food corner where she helps herself to some bread, cheese, and cheap wine.

*Ah, the sacrifices one makes to uncover the truth!*

Sipping her second glass, she looks around. The improvised dance floor is now packed with people. Roughly half pair up to dance *le roc* to a rhythmic song that blends several musical styles. The other half dance whatever they fancy and however they please. Everybody is enjoying themselves just as Katia wanted them to.

Rose is about to join the dancers when she overhears a perplexing remark from a small group engaged in an animated debate by the wall. Her antennas perk up.

"We claim we're going to improve the lives of the disenfranchised, and all that," a black man with a neat beard is saying to a pretty, young blonde. "But we just shot ourselves in the foot."

A third man, his shoulder-length blond hair tied in a low ponytail is listening with a slightly detached air. The men are about the same age as Mikel. The woman can't be more than thirty. They were keeping their voices down up until that impassioned statement, but they switch to hushed tones again. To make sure she can hear the reply, Rose sidles to the end of the food table closest to the trio.

The blonde puts a hand on her hip. "I have no idea what you mean, Lionel. Everybody is so motivated! Everybody is working their tails off so that we can do exactly what we've committed to do."

*OK, so the bearded guy's name is Lionel.*

"Except, we won't be able to do it now, will we?" Lionel gives her a defiant look.

The blonde shrugs. "I don't see why not."

"Because we accepted a lot of money from Blaise Gimbert, one of the privileged, rotten, above-the-law oligarchs we purport to fight," Lionel says.

*Ooh, he knows about Blaise's donations, and he disapproves!*

Rose serves herself a big wedge of creamy goat cheese and forks a teeny-weeny morsel. To her delight, the debate has attracted Mikel and Katia's attention who insert themselves into the group.

"So what?" the ponytail man says to Lionel. "What matters is that we're going to use that money for our cause."

Lionel lets out a bitter laugh. "How can you, all of you, including Louise, Katia, Mikel be so naïve?"

"We aren't naïve," the pretty blonde, who must be Louise, protests. "We're pragmatic."

Lionel shifts his gaze to her. "Meaning?"

"Meaning, we'll use that money to get PRAC into the parliament, government and maybe even presidency, and then we'll limit the privileges and power that the ultrarich enjoy," Louise explains. "Blaise Gimbert will be no exception!"

To Rose's surprise, Katia rolls her eyes. It lasts a split second, and no one else seems to notice it before Katia reverts to her regular mien.

Lionel shakes his head. "You're old enough to know that he who pays the piper calls the tune. Always!"

"Lionel isn't entirely wrong here," Mikel says unexpectedly. "And that is why I'm doing all I can to diversify PRAC's donor pool and sources of revenue."

Louise gawks at Mikel, awestruck. "That's so strategic! You've already envisaged this issue and are taking action! Then again, why am I surprised?"

That earns her another quick eye roll from Katia.

Her husband, on the other hand, waves Louise off half-heartedly, mumbling with false modesty, "Please, no need to praise me for just doing my job!"

"There is every need!" Louise insists. "You're brilliant, and dedicated, and you work so hard, and"—her eyes darting to Katia—"you don't get nearly enough credit for it."

Katia maintains a pleasant expression, but she balls her hands into fists.

*Come on, punch her! Make my sacrifice for missing the banquet worth it!*

"My sister is right," the ponytail guy says. "Mikel

deserves more recognition from us for everything he's achieved so far. I propose we drink to his accomplishments!"

He grabs a bottle of wine and some disposable glasses, which he fills and hands out.

Louise raises her glass, her eyes riveted to Mikel's. "Like Sammy said, we must celebrate you more. To our leader, Mikel Poupon!"

"Thank you!" Mikel seems genuinely moved. "I won't fail you, I won't fail PRAC members, and I won't fail our voters."

"I don't doubt that," Louise says.

Mikel turns to Lionel. "I'm incorruptible, my friend. Elinor knew that. She believed in me."

Several people nod.

Lionel's eyes well up as he holds Mikel's gaze. "Yes, she did."

*Who is Elinor?*

Mikel drinks. The others do the same.

Lionel wipes his lips. "Since we're toasting, here's to Elinor Hugonet!"

His booming voice draws some of the dancers and people from nearby clusters to his group. From the way they look at him and raise their glasses, it seems like many of them knew Elinor, and appreciated her.

*Wait—did Lionel say "Hugonet"?* Like the original coleader of PRAC, Dany Hugonet? Was she his widow? His daughter? Granddaughter?

Lionel's gaze becomes unfocused. "My Elinor was the smartest, purest, sweetest person I ever knew. A rising star of French journalism. My love, my partner, my..." His voice cracks. "No one will ever replace her."

*How touching!*

Considering Lionel's age, Elinor must've been Dany's granddaughter.

Katia gives his arm a gentle squeeze. "She was the best of us."

The big group around Lionel and Mikel drinks to Elinor. Rose joins them, relieved to graduate from sneaky eavesdropping to legitimate listening.

While everyone drinks, their heads tipped backward, Mikel and Katia trade a look just as quick and private as the one before.

*Do they know something about Elinor that the others don't? How did she die, by the way?*

"Hey, Mikel, do a speech!" someone calls from the crowd. "I love your speeches!"

Mikel and Katia scan the faces around them. The man raises a helpful hand.

"This isn't a rally, Nono," Katia says to him with a smile. "Tonight, we want you to relax and have fun."

Nono begins to clap rhythmically. "Speech! Speech! Speech!"

Others join him and seconds later, the entire room is clamoring for a speech.

Obviously pleased with himself, Mikel strides to the center. Rose slinks into the open spot next to Katia.

Mikel clears his throat.

He begins his speech by recounting a life-changing conversation he had with his grandfather Etienne. He waxes lyrical about Etienne's vision for a free and just society, where everyone is a master of their destiny. That's the kind of society, Mikel says, in which he wants his child to grow up in. He concludes by making a solemn promise that under his leadership, PRAC will deliver on every single promise they've made as a matter of honor.

Strangely, Mikel's words appear to suck out the joy from Katia's face.

*Why?* It's hard to believe she wouldn't want her husband

to build a better society. On the other hand, it's easy to imagine she wouldn't want him to do it with Louise by his side.

When he's done, the room erupts in applause. Rose claps, too. *He's a good speaker, Mikel.* Charismatic, articulate, handsome. He's going places.

Lionel refills his glass, drinks up, then trains his gaze on Mikel. "I hope you mean what you said. I hope you won't sell your soul, like other politicians."

"I won't," Mikel promises solemnly.

"The puppet masters will do everything to own you," Lionel warns him. "You must resist!"

Louise snorts, "Oh please, stop being such a drama queen!"

Mikel skews a tense, jerky smile. "Go easy on the wine, eh?"

"I'm done drinking for tonight," Lionel says. "I just want to say that Elinor believed in you, despite you know what. And so, I will, too!"

*What is he referring to? Blaise Gimbert's tainted money?*

Unsteady on his feet, Lionel steps closer to Mikel. "Talk is easy. Everybody talks the talk, and then cheats behind their voters' backs. Walking the walk is the hard part."

"Truth," someone in the crowd says.

Another voice joins in, "Hear, hear!"

Many nod.

"Like I said, I'm incorruptible," Mikel asserts.

Lionel grips his shoulder. "The cards are stacked against you, Mik. Your integrity will be tested. Are you solid enough to play against the house?"

"I am!" Mikel cries, lifting his chin.

Among the cheers, Rose hears Katia mutter, "The house always wins."

# CHAPTER 16

*a*fter breakfast, Rose breaks from her group again and returns to her hotel room. Her excuse this time is the looming exams. Her online PI course is demanding, and she needs to study.

While that statement is perfectly accurate, Rose hasn't been studying nearly as much as she should. Always too busy with her various hobbies, obligations, committees and clubs, Rose has been finding it increasingly hard to keep up with the program. She's begun toying with the idea that at her pace she might need an extra year to complete the course.

Alone in her room, Rose briefly considers studying, but it's much more fun to search the web for Elinor Hugonet. That's what she does. Then she calls Annie and reports diligently on everybody she met at last night's PRAC fete, and on everything that went down.

"Were you able to establish how Elinor died?" Annie asks.

"All I could gather from the eulogies I found is that it was a tragic domestic accident."

"Of what nature?"

"Unclear," Rose says. "After Mikel's speech last night, I

danced and flirted with him to extract more info, but he was very tight-lipped."

"Did you just say 'flirt'?"

"What's wrong with that?" Rose shrugs. "I wasn't going to steal him from his wife, was I? Married men have always been my redline."

"Because, otherwise, he stood no chance."

Rose can hear the derision in Annie's voice, and she doesn't like it.

"His wife Katia looked at least five years older than him," she points out. "And he didn't appear to be attracted to Louise."

"Louise... that's the eager young activist, right?"

"Yes." Rose replays their interactions in her mind. "He was flattered by her praise, for sure. But he didn't seem to be falling for her seduction. Yeah, he's definitely into older women."

Annie mutters something inaudible.

"How come you're such an old-fashioned prude?" Rose inquires. "Were you hiding under a rock during the sexual revolution?"

"I was raising my girls, which is the best thing I've done with my life."

Rose checks the train tickets on the narrow desk. "So, my TGV back to Arles leaves at six in the evening. Is there anyone else I can talk to while I'm in Paris?"

"The only person I can think of is Bernadette's best friend, Marie," Annie says. "She was an amiable, easygoing sort."

"But you don't know if she's still alive, right?"

"Women tend to live longer than men," Annie points out.

"True, but I really don't see how we could find her without a photo or a last name..."

"I have an idea!" Annie exclaims. "How didn't I think of it earlier? I'll ask Gabriel to look it up."

"You think he can run a search for 'Marie in Paris' and find her?" Rose sneers. "That won't work, darling. Take it from an almost professional PI."

"I know," Annie says.

"Then what do you mean by *looking up?*"

"A few years ago, I got Gabriel to put in a request to see René's file."

Rose didn't expect that. "Was it granted?"

"Yes, because the communication delay period, as they call it, had expired," Annie explains. "The Parisian police found the file in the archive and sent Gabriel a copy."

"Why didn't you tell me earlier?"

"Didn't I?" Annie puffs. "I thought I had. Old age truly sucks!"

"Is that how you knew the details about Grégoire's murder and René's suicide?"

"Yes," Annie says. "In '61, no one had shared that information with me, as you can imagine."

"I did wonder how you knew so much..."

Annie lets out a little laugh. "No special abilities here, unfortunately. But back to Marie. I'm sure she was interviewed at one point or another as a witness in Grégoire's murder."

"Which means Gabriel can find her name and old address in the file," Rose finishes for her.

They hang up shortly afterward.

A half-hour later, Annie calls back with Marie's full name and street address. To Rose's astonishment, the online phone book has a person with the same name still living at that address. What's more, there's a phone number to a landline.

Rose calls it.

Marie picks up and turns out to be as friendly and communicative as Annie described her. She'd be happy to meet with Rose on such a short notice and share everything she remembers about the ill-starred circle of friends from her Sciences Po days.

# CHAPTER 17

*R*ose steps off the bus to the stark Montparnasse Tower looming above her. She gives it a cursory glance, unimpressed. The graceless tower, particularly bleak on a gray day like this, has always struck her as out of place amid the classical charm of Paris. She turns her back to it, recalling Maupassant's quip about the Eiffel Tower. The writer, who had opposed its construction, despised that "eyesore" with all his heart. But he often went there for lunch, claiming it was the only place in Paris from which he couldn't see it.

He'd probably pass out at the sight of the Montparnasse Tower.

Rushing away from it, Rose heads down the Boulevard Edgar Quinet. Lined with leafless trees, the boulevard is a welcome contrast to the stark tower. The air is humid and frosty in that bone-chilling northern way that even the scent of roasting chestnuts from a nearby vendor can't redeem. Rose pulls her coat tighter around her.

As she turns onto the narrow rue d'Odessa, a lovely lineup of quaint restaurants and *crêperies* greet her. In the late nineteenth century, the impoverished Bretons came to Paris in droves in search of work. They got off the train at Montparnasse station, and some settled in the area around it. Their culinary legacy lives on in this quartier in the form of Breton crêperies that specialize in savory pancakes made with buckwheat.

A few blocks farther down the street Rose spots her destination. A string of garden lights decorates the crêperie's painted wood façade. What with the sky being so murky, the lights have already come on. Must be solar, Rose deduces. A layer of mist fogs up the windows, blurring the interior. Combined with the lights, it gives the place a glowing, mysterious warmth.

Rose pushes open the door, and a bell jingles in greeting. She's a little early, which means Marie may not have arrived yet. But that's all right. Rose can order a drink and review the questions she's going to ask.

As she shuts the door behind her, the nutty aroma of crepes sizzling in the kitchen wraps around Rose like a duvet. Waiting for a server to notice her, she studies the walls covered with vintage black-and-white photo prints of Brittany —a nod to the crêperie's roots.

A server approaches her. "*Bonjour, madame*! Do you have a reservation?"

"Yes, a table for two under Rose Tassy."

He informs her that her friend is already there, pointing to a table where a woman in her eighties is nursing a steaming mug in her hands. They wave at each other. Rose sheds her coat and makes her way to the table.

"Marie?" she says when she's close enough.

The woman nods. "And you are Rose, I assume."

With the introductions out of the way, Rose slides into the seat across from Marie. "What a cozy place!"

"I live in the neighborhood," Marie says. "This is my favorite hangout."

The server from before shows up. They order buckwheat galettes—the classic combination of cheese, ham, and egg. The server nods, scribbles down their order, and hurries away.

"You said over the phone that a friend asked you to look into Grégoire's and René's deaths," Marie begins. "May I ask who that friend is?"

"Annie Malian."

"Annie..." Marie's eyes light up. "Wait, I know! Is she the young woman from Marseilles that visited René in 1960, I think? We spent a lovely day roaming the Latin Quarter together."

"The very same." Rose grins. "She's eighty-four now."

"Me too. How time flies!" Marie's gaze grows distant. "I remember those days... We were so young, so full of life and dreams!"

Rose leans forward. "What can you tell me about René and his relationship with Grégoire and Bernadette? You and Bernadette were close, weren't you?"

"Oh, yes."

"Was there a love triangle between her, Grégoire, and René?"

Marie shakes her head. "Bernadette was smitten with Grégoire, you know. He was quite the charmer."

"And René?" Rose asks. "Do you think he could've been secretly into Bernadette?"

"He was fond of her, as a friend, but he wasn't interested in her romantically."

"Are you certain?"

Marie takes a sip of her tea. "I always suspected he had a girl back home in Marseilles. When Annie paid him a visit, I had my answer."

The galettes arrive, golden and crisp with the cheese

melted just so and the egg cooked to perfection. The aroma is mouthwatering. Rose can't help but dig in at once.

Marie goes on, her voice barely rising above the background chatter of the crêperie. "They never said they were an item, but the way they looked at each other, the way he fussed over her... It stared you in the face."

"They were secretly engaged," Rose informs her.

"See? I knew it!"

"Did you get a chance to tell the investigators at the time what you're telling me now?" Rose asks. "That René wasn't interested in Bernadette?"

She confirms with several eager nods. "Bernadette told them the same thing. But the commissaire in charge had credible witnesses who claimed René was obsessed with Bernadette."

"Who were those witnesses?"

Marie spreads her hands. "I have no idea, but the police chose to believe them over us."

"That's odd."

"Isn't it? I honestly think those testimonies were fake."

This piece of information sets two parallel trains of thought in Rose's mind. Desperately, she tries to keep track of both. The first one is obvious. Thanks to René's file that Gabriel has access to, it should be possible to determine who those witnesses were. It's almost certain they'd lied to the police. And that makes them suspicious.

The second idea that came to Rose is trickier to catch. It had something to do with a qualifier Marie used... Fake. Someone else connected to this case recently used a similar epithet in relation to a person who didn't deserve it... *Jacques!*

He called René a fraud during the post-quiz dinner in Le Crotoy. Throughout the meal, he kept dropping hints that his brother had been a bad man, and that the family's financial ruin had had something to do with René's "shady dealings."

Jacques didn't specify which. His sister Monique assumed Jacques was referring to René's involvement with PRAC.

At the time, Rose knew nothing about PRAC, so she went with Monique's theory. But now she knows that PRAC opposed capitalism as fervently in the sixties as it does now. It follows that a wealthy family wouldn't be thrilled to find out that one of theirs joined such a movement. But to call René's activism with PRAC "shady dealings" is a stretch.

*What if it wasn't René's politics that Jacques was hinting at, but at something else?*

Rose takes the final bite of her galette and lets its flavors melt on her tongue.

Her eyes are half-shut, partly in pleasure and partly to formulate her next question. "Tell me... during the time that you knew René, was he mixed up in any clandestine activities, other than PRAC that is?"

"Not that I know of. He was a good sort, you know? Him murdering Grégoire never made sense to me."

"You and Annie are on the same page about René." Rose chews on her lip. "But when we talked to his brother, he mentioned René's shady dealings."

"What shady dealings?"

"He didn't elaborate," Rose says. "I was hoping you'd be able to shed some light."

"Well, there was one episode that comes to mind..."

Rose raises an eyebrow. "What episode?"

"I don't know if I should mention it." Marie thumbs her ear. "It was so out of character for René that it seemed unreal. I must've misinterpreted what I saw."

Rose narrows her eyes. "What did you see? It could be important, Marie!"

"It isn't."

Rose hikes an eyebrow in question.

"I did tell the police about it at the time," Marie says.

"They said it was unrelated to the case. To this day, I feel guilty about marring René's image for something I likely misunderstood."

"But what if you didn't?" Rose stares Marie in the eye. "Also, the cops were wrong about René's feelings for Bernadette, weren't they? What if they were wrong about this, too?"

"I'd hate to repeat the same mistake and soil Annie's memory of René for nothing."

A waitress clears their table and asks if they'd like sweet crepes for dessert. Rose picks the one with blackberry jam, and Marie, the Chef's special.

"All Annie wants is to uncover the truth of what happened to her first love," Rose says. "It's the only item on her bucket list."

"But what if my anecdote leads her away from the truth?"

Rose leans back in her chair. "We have nothing else to go on. So, wherever your anecdote takes us is going to be better than getting nowhere."

The waitress brings their desserts. Rose takes a bite, letting the sweet, happy taste of the crepe fill her mouth.

*Fingers crossed Marie spills the beans! I don't know what else to say to persuade her.*

Marie doesn't touch her crepe. She looks at Rose, her expression tortured. Then, suddenly, her features smooth out. She sweeps her hand over her face. "In the fall of 1960, I witnessed a very unusual incident from afar."

Rose stops eating. "Go on."

"Two men approached René outside of Sciences Po. They showed him some photographs. René seemed upset. They argued, but I couldn't make out what they were saying."

Rose holds her breath.

"When they realized they were drawing attention," Marie continues, "the men nudged René toward their car.

He got in and they drove off. René was gone for over a week."

"Did he say where he'd been when he got back?"

"He said he'd gone home to Marseilles for some family emergency." She curls her lip. "His dad wrote a long letter to the faculty administration, explaining why he'd called his son by his side."

"What was his reason?"

"Something health related. Except I don't think it was true."

Rose squints at her. "Why would you say that?"

"Because..." Marie hesitates again.

Rose picks up her fork and knife to occupy herself. *Please, don't change your mind! Don't deny me the reveal!*

"I believe I recognized one of the men who'd whisked René away," Marie finally says.

Rose's fork pauses midair. "Who was he?"

"Barthelemy 'Mémé' Leoni," Marie says, like it's supposed to shock Rose.

Rose blinks. "Who?"

"Oh, come on, he was on the front page of all the papers at least once a month in the fifties and early sixties! Don't you remember?"

"I wasn't born yet," Rose says.

Marie sizes Rose up.

*OK, OK, I was already born. But I was a child!*

The eight years that Marie has on Rose change everything. Both Marie and Annie are pre-World War II babies. The year 1960 was the peak of their youth. Rose, on the other hand, is a boomer. Her heyday didn't begin until 1968. It's the braless disco seventies, and not the big hair rock'n'roll sixties, that was the best and wildest decade of her life.

"Mémé Leoni was one of the most prominent and extravagant figures of Le Milieu," Marie says.

"Are you referring to the Corsican mob?"

Marie nods. "Yes. In those days, they operated mostly out of Marseilles as a decentralized criminal syndicate everybody called the French Connection."

"Heroin dealers, right?"

"Right. They ran sophisticated drug labs, excelled at money laundering, corruption, violence—you name it."

Rose knits her eyebrows. "So, you saw René, our good boy from a good family, arguing and getting into a car with a notorious mobster and some other guy and then lying about the reason for his absence?"

"Assuming it was Mémé Leoni that I saw. But I could be wrong."

"Assuming it was him, what do you think René had gotten mixed up in?"

"I'm afraid I can't help you there," Marie says apologetically. "I haven't got the slightest idea."

"That's all right," Rose reassures her. "You've been immensely helpful."

*She really was.*

Rose's mind is already racing with possibilities, each more sensational than the last.

# CHAPTER 18

$\mathcal{A}$nnie's living room in Cassis is filled with the soft coos of baby Maxime. Annie holds him close, all her aches forgotten. She talks to him in that universal language of doting adults in which the tone is more important than the words. Maxime, all round cheeks and dimples, grabs Annie's gold necklace with his chubby little fingers.

Edwige is sitting on the couch, making small talk with Rose.

"You're Annie's younger daughter's daughter-in-law, right?" Rose asks her.

"That's right, I'm David's wife," Edwige says. "We live in Cassis, too, so it's easy to stop by and let Medz Mama and baby Max have some cozy time together."

Annie shoots a grateful look at Edwige. "In a few days, it's going to be our family's first Catholic and then Orthodox Christmas with a new generation around. You have no idea how much joy it brings me!"

"We're all very excited," Edwige says to Rose. "I already bought him a little Santa suit."

116

"How adorable!" Rose's gaze lingers on the baby. "Just make sure he doesn't try to climb up the chimney in it."

Edwige laughs, instinctively reaching out to touch Maxime's soft hair. "I'll keep that in mind."

The clock on the wall strikes five.

Edwige glances at it and stands up. "We should get going."

*Already?* Hiding her reluctance, Annie hands Max over to his mom, her fingers lingering on his soft cheek for a moment longer.

Edwige leans over to kiss Annie goodbye before strapping Max into the baby carrier. Rose waves to them. Edwige waves back, wishing her a merry Christmas.

As the door closes behind them, Rose glances at Annie. "Ah, *pichoons*," she says in Provençal, her voice soft. "What is it about babies that makes everything better?"

Annie grins. "Where do I begin?"

"The mushiness? The gurgles? The smell?"

"I hope you don't mean the diaper smell!" Annie adds with a smile before she touches Rose's hand. "Sorry again for making you drive all the way to Cassis. I might be unable to walk for a week or more."

"It was no trouble at all," Rose says, pouring them both some tea from the pot.

Annie was supposed to meet Rose in Beldoc, but her knee pain flared up, turning her into the Little Mermaid again. *What was it that the Sea Witch said to the Little Mermaid in Andersen's tale?* "Every step you take will feel as if you were treading upon knife blades..."

Anyway, Rose kindly agreed to come over to Cassis, where Annie lives with her daughter Claire and her son-in-law George, so that they could plan their next moves. When Rose arrived, Annie came down to the living room. Claire served tea with baklava pastries. Edwige dropped in with

Maxime to say hi, after which Annie and Rose were left to their own devices.

Annie raises her teacup. "Old age sucks. Why can't we stay young forever?"

"Some of us manage longer than others," Rose says smugly.

*You don't take prisoners, do you?*

Funnily enough, Rose's tactless remark doesn't rile Annie as much as it would've a week ago. Has she gotten used to Rose's ways? Grown thicker skin? Glimpsed an unexpected warmth behind the hippie diva's ostentatious façade? It's hard to tell.

"There's a flip side to growing old, though," Annie says.

Rose scoffs. "No, there isn't."

"Think about it," Annie urges her. "When I was young, I needed things to happen for me to feel happy. Special things. Now, the mere absence of pain anywhere in my body is enough."

Rose humphs as if to show she isn't convinced. "Shall I tell you about my conversation with Marie?"

"Yes, please."

Rose recounts her lunch at the Montparnasse crêperie. Annie takes notes.

When Rose is done, she points at Annie's scratch pad. "Make a note to ask Gabriel to check who the witnesses were that told the police that René carried a torch for Bernadette."

"Will do."

"On my end, I'll get Julie and Flo to research the mobster Mémé Leoni, and the French Connection. If we're lucky, he's still alive."

Annie picks up a bite-size pastry. "Shouldn't you do the research yourself? Julie has a full-time job."

"I'm sure she'll be happy to give us a hand," Rose says.

"Did you hear her complain when she helped us after the trip to Le Crotoy? Gabriel didn't complain either."

"No, but—"

Rose interrupts her, "Do you want to uncover the truth about René, yes or no?"

"I want nothing more!"

"Then we ask for all the help we can get. Julie and Flo are much better at Internet research than I will ever be."

Annie can relate to that. "Computers scare the hell out of me."

"A good PI, like a good manager, is aware of her limits and knows when to delegate."

Annie gives up. "You're right."

"Which brings me to a tricky question." Rose reaches for another pastry. "You won't like it, but as a diligent detective, it is my duty to ask."

"Ask away."

"Is it possible that René was mixed up with Le Milieu?"

Annie narrows her eyes. "Like, did he work for them? Why would he do that? He had principles, and he didn't need the money."

"What if he was a gambler? No one is without sin."

"René was without sin," Annie says. "He was the purest soul I ever knew."

"Imagine he lost tons of money in a gambling den," Rose carries on, ignoring Annie's statement. "He was too ashamed to tell his dad. So, he borrowed from the Mob to pay his debts, which gave the Mob leverage over him."

Annie shakes her head. "Impossible."

"All right. OK. I thought you'd say that." Rose refills her teacup. "Let me ask you a different question. Do you recall a time in the Chantomes' life that fits with Marie's story? Had René ever disappeared and then reappeared? Had he gone radio silent for a week?"

"I spoke with him only once a week, and so did his parents," Annie says. "This was normal before individual cell phones."

"I know. I'm young, but not *that* young."

In a sudden flash of memory, Annie recalls something. "One morning, while cleaning the house, I realized that René was in his room. He'd arrived the night before on an unplanned visit outside of school holidays. He looked like he'd been run over."

"When was that?"

"In the fall of 1960."

"That's when Marie saw René get into a car with Mémé Leoni!" Rose exclaims.

"He said he'd had a bicycle accident, nothing broken but a mild concussion and lots of bruising."

"The mobsters must've roughed him up."

In her mind's eye, Annie sees René in his bed, propped by pillows. His swollen face is illuminated by a melancholy smile as he talks to her.

"He told me he was on a weeklong sick leave."

"And you didn't ask any further questions?"

Annie spreads her hands. "I was too happy to see him, and his story didn't strike me as improbable."

For the next five minutes, Annie and Rose drink their tea in silence. Annie's thoughts have drifted far away, to the fall of 1960. To anchor them in the present again, she focuses on the Provençal santon figurines of the Christmas manger by the wall, and then on the oriental pastries before her. They glisten with syrup, their phyllo dough topped with finely chopped nuts. She picks up a sticky piece and bites into it, meditating on the gentle crunch of the nuts.

Rose slaps her forehead. "I forgot to mention an interesting detail when I told you about the PRAC fete over the phone."

"I'm all ears."

"Mikel Poupon's wife Katia acted weird."

"In what way?"

Rose screws up her face. "Repressed antagonism? Lack of faith in her husband? Or maybe she was just pissed at Louise's adulation of him."

Annie changes her position to relieve the aching knee. "I agree it's interesting, but I don't see how it's relevant to our case."

"Me neither," Rose admits. "OK, here's the other thing. Remember Elinor Hugonet, the journalist who died in a tragic domestic accident six months ago?"

"Granddaughter of Dany Hugonet, the second-in-command at the original PRAC?"

Rose nods. "Her boyfriend Lionel reproached Mikel for taking the Gimberts' money. Lionel's concern is that, if elected, Mikel would be beholden to Blaise Gimbert."

"Can a political party refuse a donation?" Annie asks.

"I don't think so. But if Mikel had made it super clear to Blaise to expect zero favors or special treatment, I doubt PRAC would've received the maximum authorized amount from every family member of Blaise."

Rose's words spark an idea in Annie's mind. "You say Elinor was a journalist..."

"Yes."

"Remember when we went to Monaco with Noam? Blaise told him he wasn't the first journalist to think the Gimberts' sponsorship of PRAC was a scoop?"

Rose's eyes light up. "And he wouldn't tell us who that other journalist was! What if it was Elinor? Oh my God, what if she was going to go public with her story before she died?"

They stare at each other.

"You should find Lionel's number and give him a call," Annie says.

ANA T. DREW

"On what pretext?"

"Refer to the things he said at the fete and tell him how they stayed with you."

Rose smiles. "They did, as a matter of fact."

"Then you won't be lying."

Rose stands up. "I'll see what I can do. And, thank you so much for the tea and the delicious pastries—"

"You're staying for dinner," Annie cuts her off.

"That's very nice of you, but I don't want to outstay my welcome."

"Rubbish. You're staying."

Cautiously, Rose asks, "Is there a special reason?"

"Claire is making dolma." Annie taps her nose. "Can you smell it?"

Rose sniffs the air. "Matter of fact, I can! It's a Greek dish, isn't it?"

"Everybody in the region has their variant of it," Annie says. "But the Armenians do it best."

"Of course."

Annie snarls. "I'm serious. The Armenian dolma, and Claire's in particular, is incomparable."

Rose lifts an eyebrow at the hyperbole.

"Here is how you must eat it," Annie says. "First, you'll focus on the textures against your tongue. You'll feel the smoothness of the eggplant, the ribs of the cabbage leaf, the crumbly softness of the tomato. Do it before the flavors steal your attention. The ripe vegetables, fresh meat, rice, basil, salt, and black pepper, all perfectly dosed and cooked. Incomparable."

"I didn't realize you wrote poetry."

"Only about food."

Rose chuckles. "I know someone else who gets all poetic about food."

"Julie?" Annie shrugs smugly. "She'll do."

If she were completely truthful, she would've told Rose she prays every day for her grandson to get his shit together, marry Rose's granddaughter, and have their first baby while she's alive. But she fears she'd come across as too intense if she says that aloud.

# CHAPTER 19

*E*nsconced in the passenger seat, Annie adjusts the scarf around her neck but doesn't dare turn up the heat. Oblivious to Annie's discomfort, Rose navigates her bright yellow Nissan through the winding streets of Roquevaire, a village twenty kilometers northeast of Cassis. Annie peers out, her breath fogging up the glass.

"Look at that!" Rose points her gloved hand toward the town hall.

A vibrant Christmas tree stands tall in front of the stone building, its rich green and red baubles a beacon of warmth against the gray winter sky.

As they pass the tree, Annie lets her eyes follow the trail of colorful ornaments.

"Beautiful," she says.

As recently as two days ago, Annie didn't think she'd be able to make this short trip. But over the last forty-eight hours, her knee flare-up subsided, and she decided to tag along with Rose. On this bleak winter solstice day, the two of them are about to pay a visit to a potential suspect, retired gangster Napoleon "Big Napo" Albertini.

Julie and Flo did a terrific job tracking down all the former members of Le Milieu still alive. From that small pool, they singled out Big Napo for several reasons. First, he was one of Mémé Leoni's young lieutenants in the late fifties. That means he could've been the man Marie saw helping Mémé abduct René.

Mémé's boss in the criminal hierarchy was his older brother Paul Leoni, one of godfathers of the Marseillais Milieu. The Leoni brothers were long dead. But Big Napo, now eighty-six, was still standing and well enough to live on his own. And in Provence, as luck would have it.

Annie still can't believe that he agreed to talk to them. In fact, he sounded delighted at the prospect, according to Rose.

Squinting at the street signs, Rose grumbles something about the pain of finding the address with all the road work and detours. Finally, on the outer rim of the village, they find the street and the house.

An old codger in aviator sunglasses, his bald skull shiny and his swarthy face deeply creased, opens the gate. Rose parks the car. Annie waits for Rose to come and give her a hand, but it's Big Napo who rushes to her side.

"May I?" he asks Annie, offering a flexed arm as a prop.

She grips it. "Thank you!"

As he leads them across the cluttered yard, Annie hears hens clucking and the rustle of straw. Then she spots a chicken coop. There's a familiar smell in the air.

"Monsieur Albertini," she says to the reformed mobster, "Fresh eggs?"

"Indeed, madame." He surveys her face. "I'm guessing you're Annie Malian."

"Did my nose gave me away?" Annie asks with a smile.

He gives a hearty laugh. "It's a magnificent nose. Full of character. Unmissable."

*That's what René used to say!*

"You can call me Annie," she offers, surprising herself.

"I'd be delighted to, Annie." He turns to Rose. "And you must be Rose Tassy."

"The one and only," Rose says.

He grins. "And, please, ladies, call me Napo. I went by Big Napo back in the day, but I dropped the *big* after I served my second sentence."

*Thank you for reminding me about who you are!*

Annie averts her gaze, ashamed she was beginning to like this man, a former gangster potentially implicated in René's kidnapping and death.

Rose points at the coop. "You're hatching chicks in winter. How odd!"

Napo laughs again, his vivacious eyes crinkling behind the sunglasses. "Are you aware that hens don't hibernate? They can lay eggs all year round."

He leads them into his house and shuts the door behind them. A pleasant warmth envelops Annie as she steps inside. While Napo swaps his sunglasses for regular spectacles, Annie looks around. In the corner of the spacious entryway, a brooder hums softly. A cluster of fluffy yellow chicks peeps inside. Napo picks up one of them.

Its tiny body nestled in his calloused hands, he explains, "See, incubating is essentially the same in the winter as it is in the spring. You just need to make some adjustments."

"Like what?" Annie asks.

He gestures to the machine next to the brooder. "I let the eggs sit overnight before placing them into the incubator. And, as you can see, I move the brooder into the house to protect the young ones from the cold."

"You learn something new every day," Rose murmurs, her gaze lingering on the brooder.

"That's the beauty of life, isn't it?" Napo retorts. "Always full of surprises."

*Have you found Jesus or is this all an act?* Annie itches to ask.

How can this gracious, good-humored, chicken-breeding fellow be a notorious mobster who committed all sorts of crimes in his youth and served two terms in prison for them? Can people change that profoundly? Or is he a gentleman thief who stops to hold the door for a woman on his way to robbing a bank?

"Follow me," Napo says, leading them to the kitchen, the chick still in his hands.

The room, though small, is impeccably neat with every item in its rightful place. The countertops are devoid of clutter, save for a few essential appliances—a kettle, a toaster, and an Italian espresso maker with two chambers. The Formica cabinets must be from the last century, but they're in mint state. The spotless black-and-white floor tiles reflect the care Napo gives to his home despite his advanced years, the chicks in his entryway, and the hens in his yard.

A wooden table flanked by four matching chairs sits in the center of the room. The scent of fresh coffee permeates the air.

"I just brewed a pot," Napo says, pulling a chair for Annie and then Rose. "May I offer you a cup?"

Both women nod, and he pours them coffee with one hand while still holding the chick in his other.

Napo sits down. "Rose said on the phone you had questions about René Chantome."

"He was my fiancé," Annie says.

"That poor kid, so unfortunate!" Napo shakes his head. "Such a messy, tragic ending for such an upstanding guy! *Actually* upstanding, unlike his father."

The implications of Napo's intro are so big that Annie's neurons go into overdrive. Her mind boggles, and she freezes up, unable to move or speak. Even thinking becomes an insurmountable effort.

Gabriel has an expression for when this happens: Medz Mama is rebooting. Annie is unclear what *rebooting* means, but she can sense it will take a while this time.

# CHAPTER 20

*F*ortunately for Annie, Rose appears to have retained her self-command after Napo's mini scoop.

She trains her eyes on him. "Are you suggesting that Pierre-François Chantome worked for the Mob? Was he an auctioneer by day and *truand* by night? Was René's kidnapping in Paris linked to his father's activities?"

"What about René's death?" Annie asks, finally pulling herself together. "Did one of your friends kill Grégoire Lacaze, frame René for it, and then kill him, too?"

"Whoa! I know nothing about that," Napo protests.

Rose speaks in a voice much calmer than Annie's, "OK, just tell us what you do know."

"With pleasure." He takes a sip of coffee. "Hmm, where do I begin?"

"At the beginning," Rose suggests.

His lips quirk. "I believe I'll kick off with a brief historical overview."

"Is it necessary?" Annie smiles pleasantly to conceal her impatience.

"Back in the fifties," Napo says, "the Corsican and Marseillais Milieu collaborated with the French secret services."

Annie frowns. "Aren't the Mob and the government supposed to be sworn enemies?"

"Have you heard the saying, 'The enemy of my enemy is my friend'?" he asks.

"Who was their common enemy?" Rose inquires.

Napo caresses the chick's head with his finger. "The commies and the trade unions dominated by the commies."

"I still don't get it," Rose says. "What bone did the gangsters have to pick with the communists and the trade unions?"

"Good question, Rose!" Napo strokes his own head now, using all five fingers. "Many unionized dockers had refused to load weapons for the French army fighting a colonial war in Indochina. The authorities fired eight hundred of them. In retaliation, four thousand dockers went on strike in March 1950."

"How was that bad for Le Milieu?" Annie asks.

"The ports were blocked," he replies. "That was very bad for our business because we needed the base that came from Turkey to make our flour from. We couldn't move our merchandise to the US, either."

Annie meshes her hands together. "When you speak of base and flour those aren't baking terms, are they?"

"Apologies for the jargon, Annie! The base stands for morphine, and the flour is one of heroin's many names."

Rose looks him up and down, her gaze lingering on the fluffy thing in his hands. "Are we to understand that you and your friends engaged in transatlantic heroin trade?"

"Le Milieu had the best labs and the most sought-after chemists, I'll have you know," Napo says with pride. "We produced ninety-eight percent pure, top-quality heroin. Best in the world."

Rose's eyebrows go up and hold. "Wow!"

"Hello?" Annie snaps her fingers in front of Rose's face. "Heroin is poison. You know that, right? It destroys lives."

Rose blinks, as if waking up from a dream. "Of course."

Annie turns to Napo. "I'm assuming the authorities used the gangsters to break the strike."

"Bingo!" he exclaims. "The government made a deal with Godfather Paul Leoni and his younger brother Mémé who later became my boss."

"What sort of deal?" Rose asks.

"The authorities released hundreds of gangsters from prison," Napo says.

Rose smiles. "Including you?"

"Nah, I was only thirteen in 1950."

"Did those freed gangsters replace the dockers?" Annie asks.

Napo points at her with a forefinger in a "you" gesture. "The Leoni brothers broke the strike. As a thank you, the authorities closed their eyes on their activities for most of the fifties."

"That was very educational," Annie says. "But can you tell us everything you know about René?"

"Patience, I'm getting there." He leaves the kitchen to set chick back into the chirruping brooder.

Annie takes slow breaths to steady her heart.

Napo reclaims his seat at the kitchen table. "Because Paul Leoni had a carte blanche for a while, he became a big player in the French Connection. By the late fifties, when Mémé recruited me, the clan's profits had skyrocketed."

"Did you partake in any of that bounty?" Rose asks.

"Their money did trickle down, unlike the modern billionaires' profits." His lips curve into a smile. "I owned a luxury car and two beautiful homes when I got nabbed in '62."

"Carry on," Annie urges him.

"The problem with illicit drug money is that it needs laundering before you can enjoy it," he says. "That's done through legitimate businesses serving as fronts."

Annie looks at him expectantly.

He shifts his gaze from her to Rose and then back. "Auction houses are an excellent choice. For one, they allow anonymous transactions and routinely move art pieces across borders."

"With no oversight?" Rose asks.

"Some, but much less than for direct money transfers," Napo explains. "Most importantly, because the value of art is so subjective, it can be easily inflated."

Annie stares into Napo's black eyes as the penny drops on his exposé on auction houses.

Rose seems to catch on, too, because she cries out, "Wait— René's dad laundered money for the Mob!"

"How did your bosses manage to get René's dad to agree to that?" Annie asks Napo.

"Thank you for asking!" He beams. "In 1959, Paul Leoni approached Pierre-François Chantome with a very tempting deal."

"Like the snake with the apple," Annie mutters.

Napo flashes his dentures. "The deal was, we use the Chantome auction house to launder our gains from a recent heroin sale. We do that just once, Pierre-François takes thirty percent, and then each party carries on like we don't know each other."

"Thirty percent of what amount?" Rose asks.

"That information was above my pay grade," Napo replies. "But it had been our biggest sale that year, so I imagine it was a tidy sum."

"What did Pierre-François say?" Annie knits her eyebrows. "I can't imagine he just went, 'Fantastic, laundering money for Le Milieu has always been my dream.'"

"He said no way at first. But Paul was very persuasive. And he'd picked the Chantome auction house for a reason. Few people knew it yet, but Pierre-François had lost a lot of money because his assessors had made a series of expensive mistakes."

Rose smirks. "So, he ended up agreeing to that onetime operation, didn't he?"

"Yes, he did, Rose," Napo confirms. "And we did leave him in peace for about a year. But in October 1960, the Leoni brothers found themselves in a bind, struggling to launder a sum they needed urgently to reinvest in a big shipment."

Annie cups her cheek with a woeful sigh. "And the trap closed on Pierre-François."

"We made him a great offer," Napo says. "He would become our *saraf*, our shadow banker, in exchange for thirty percent on every transaction, plus a monthly retainer."

"That's a generous offer," Rose says, earning another glare from Annie.

"Yet, Pierre-François said no!" Napo sits back. "And that's why Mémé and Dom Spirito were sent to Paris to kidnap René."

Rose leans closer. "Why kidnap René all the way in Paris when you could grab Jacques or Monique from Marseilles?"

"Because Pierre-François made it no secret that René was his favorite child," Napo replies.

Rose twists her mouth with disgust. "That's shabby parenting. No wonder Jacques is so bitter!"

"What happened next?" Annie asks.

"Next, Mémé and Dom found René, showed him some proof that his dad was working for us, and got him into their car. He was so shocked by what he saw that he hardly resisted."

Annie releases a shaggy breath. "Where did they take him?"

"To the cave, as we call it in Le Milieu. It means a safe house," Napo says. "Mémé called Pierre-François and told him that if he wanted to see René again, he must become our saraf."

Annie surveys the old man who's suddenly a lot less charming than before. "How do you know that?"

"I was present during that call. Pierre-François was sobbing, begging us not to harm René." Napo rubs his cheek. "Mémé gave him seventy-two hours. The man was devastated."

"Did he go to the police in that time?" Rose asks.

"Mémé swore to him we'd shoot René on the spot if he tried that."

"And he believed the threat?"

"He had no reason not to." Napo shrugs. "Le Milieu was known to be ruthless. That being said, we never killed gratuitously or over a trifle like today's punks. Marseilles has gone down the toilet of late."

*That's rich, coming from you!*

"Did Pierre-François become your saraf?" Annie asks.

"No, he didn't," Napo says. "He used the time we gave him to sell the auction house and liquidate all his assets. An hour before our deadline he called Mémé."

"What did he say?" Rose and Annie ask at the same time.

"He said he couldn't launder our money because he didn't have an auction house anymore."

Annie gasps.

Napo continues, "He'd sold all his holdings, his mansion and his second home. He said he'd give us all the proceeds, in cash, if we freed René."

Rose puckers her lips. "Hmm... A bold but risky move. Your boss said yes, I imagine, seeing as René was returned to his family."

"Mémé was inclined to say no," Napo points out. "But he called Paul, who said yes."

Rose squints. "Greed?"

"For sure," Napo agrees. "But also because Paul, himself a father, could appreciate the sacrifice and the boldness, as you called it, of Pierre-François's move."

"Back to the events, please," Annie prompts.

"A drop-off point was set in the outskirts of Marseilles," Napo says. "After midnight, Mémé, Dom, and I drove there with René bound and gagged in the trunk. My job was to shoot the kid in the head if it turned out we'd been ambushed."

Annie peers at him. "Were you going to go through with that?"

"Today's Napoleon Albertini wouldn't," he replies. "But the Big Napo of 1960... I would've hated myself for it, but I believe I would've done it out of loyalty to Mémé and Paul."

It's the first time in Annie's life that she's confronted with someone like Napo—a lovely man who used to be a monster.

Could it be that his second incarceration after which he dropped the "big" from his name actually did what the label said? Did it sort him out?

Napo pulls up the cross on the thick gold chain around his neck and kisses it. "Luckily for my soul, Pierre-François showed up alone without cops. He handed Mémé a briefcase chock-full of money. Mémé counted the wads. We released René."

"In what state?" Annie asks. "Had you beaten him up? When I saw him the next day, he wasn't exactly in top form."

"Aside from an occasional punch when he wouldn't do as

135

he was told, we'd inflicted no deliberate beatings or torture," Napo assures her.

Annie nods. "I believe you. He recovered within a few days."

"After that swap, we left Pierre-François and his children alone," Napo says.

"You didn't have to," Rose points out.

"Believe it or not, gangsters have a code of honor," Napo retorts. "Or, should I say, used to have."

"What else can you tell us?" Annie asks.

"That's pretty much it." He scratches the back of his head. "I heard that with the bit of money Paul allowed the Chantomes to keep, Pierre-François bought a seedy little place in the north, and the family moved there."

"Today that place is one of Le Crotoy's best hotels," Rose says. "The Chantomes worked miracles with it."

Napo smiles. "I'm glad to hear it. After Pierre-François sold everything to ransom René, I came to respect him. To us Corsicans, family is sacred. Pierre-François deserved a measure of comfort."

Annie folds her arms across her chest. "Let's recap. You, Dom Spirito, Mémé Leoni and Paul Leoni were involved in René's kidnapping in October 1960. Did you have anything to do with his death in January '61?"

"Nothing at all! Why would we kill him?"

Annie shrugs. "Out of frustration? To punish Pierre-François for escaping your clutches?"

"Pff! Mémé and Paul came to consider that man a godsend. They were so grateful for him, they often toasted to him at private feasts." Napo leans back with a take-that look on his face.

"And why would your bosses be grateful for Pierre-François Chantome?" Annie asks.

Napo moves his chair closer to them. "First and foremost,

because the guy who bought the auction house from him needed no coaxing to launder money for us. The moment the ink was dry on the contract, he reached out to us with an offer."

"And second?" Rose inquires.

Napo shifts his gaze between Rose and Annie. "Isn't it obvious?"

"No, it isn't," Annie says.

"René's unplanned ransom was our cleanest, lowest-risk, least hassle, best-value operation of all time!" With a roguish smile on his face, he sweeps a hand around the kitchen. "I bought this house with my share."

# CHAPTER 21

*R*ose deftly wraps a box of macarons for a customer. "Here you go, madame. Enjoy!"

"Oh, I'm sure we will. We love Julie's creations," the customer says before she slips out into the chilly evening.

Back in August, when Julie planned and advertised her workshops for the rest of the year, she decided to include one on gingerbread houses shortly before Christmas. That turned out to be a great idea. Despite the participation fee that was higher than average, she was unable to accommodate all the applicants, even after adding ten spots. Rose can hear them in the shop's spacious kitchen now. The workshop is going well.

What Julie hadn't factored in was how busy they'd be three days before Christmas. Typically, she closes the pâtisserie for two hours when she conducts a workshop. But with the number of customers this year, a two-hour closure would've meant losing a nice chunk of money.

That's where Rose came in. She's giving Flo a hand on the front line while Eric helps Julie as she teaches the workshop in the rear. And because Rose never lets a good deed of hers go unrewarded, she graciously accepted Julie's offer to host a case-related meeting at eight as soon as the workshop ends and the pâtisserie closes for the day. In the meantime, Gabriel will pick up Annie and bring her to the shop.

When the influx of customers slacks to a rate that Flo can manage on her own, Rose takes advantage of the respite to sidle to the kitchen door and peek in. Eager participants of all ages are huddled around the large stainless-steel table. The ambiance is light and festive, but the faces are tense with concentration.

Eric pulls out a tray of gingerbread pieces from the oven. Their rich, spicy aroma fills the room, drawing a collective sigh from the group. He sets the tray on a cooling rack.

Julie's voice carries over the chatter of the participants, "Alright, everyone! The first step to building our gingerbread house is to let these pieces cool completely. If they're warm, the icing won't stick well."

The participants nod.

She turns to Eric, a twinkle in her eye. "Royal icing, please."

"*Oui*, Chef!" he barks, fetching a piping bag filled with icing.

"This," she says, as Eric hands over the bag, "is our glue. It's what holds our houses together."

Her hand steady and sure, Julie demonstrates how to pipe a thick line of icing along the edge of one of the cooled gingerbread cutouts.

"Don't be stingy with it," she advises. "You want the bond to be strong. Just make sure to leave plenty of icing—at least a third—for the decoration."

She presses another gingerbread shape against the icing, holds it in place for a few seconds, and then repeats with another piece. The participants watch with rapt attention as she works.

*Boy, can she bake! But can she do a headstand?*

Not only can she not, but she doesn't even want to learn. For a former tree-climbing tomboy, Julie's consistent avoidance of physical exercise mystifies and saddens Rose.

*She'll end up like Annie if she doesn't watch out!*

"And there you have it," Julie says.

She steps back to admire her gingerbread house standing sturdy and proud on the table. Some of the younger participants clap.

"Now it's your turn," Julie says. "You'll each assemble a house while Eric and I walk around and give a hand anywhere it's needed."

"Aren't you going to decorate your house?" a teenage girl asks Julie.

"We all will," Julie replies. "It's the best part!"

"Rose, can you give me a hand?" Flo calls from behind the counter.

Rose rushes back to her workstation. The flow of customers stays constant after that, refusing to ebb until closing time.

AT EIGHT-TEN, the workshop participants are finally gone, each with their gingerbread house in a pretty box. While Julie and Eric clean up the kitchen, Flo tidies up the front shop. Rose peeks outside to see if Karl and Harley are around as they often are at this time of night. They are, so she gets Karl tea and a croissant and some water for Harley.

"I spoke with Victor," she says to Karl. "It's within his power to get you and Harley beds at that new shelter through March."

"Thank you!"

Rose shakes her head. "Don't thank me yet. You need to help him help you. You need to give him your real name."

Karl bites into his croissant and averts his gaze.

Rose touches his arm. "No one else needs to know it, not even me. Just the mayor. Will you tell him?"

"No," Karl says. "I'm happy on the streets. It's all good."

Rose is about to say he didn't look happy earlier this month, coughing and shaking under the bridge, when a familiar car pulls up, distracting her.

Gabriel helps Annie out.

Karl whistles to Harley and nods to Rose. "Thanks for trying, Rose; I appreciate it. But let it be."

He turns his back to her and saunters away with Harley in tow.

Rose lets Annie and Gabriel into the shop.

At eight-thirty Eric, the only male member of Julie's amateur detective group, leaves due to a prior engagement. Probably with his girlfriend. The rest gather around Annie for the much-anticipated Progress Assessment Meeting.

Rose is about to begin, when Julie flashes a palm at her and darts to the kitchen. She returns three minutes later with a tray loaded with pastries.

"Everybody," she says, "may I present the latest experiment in my bid to replace sugar with healthier natural substitutes?"

Flo gives Annie a wink. "Julie is on a mission to make her desserts not only gluten free but also guilt free."

"Natural sugar substitutes are tricky," Julie explains. "Although much better for you than sugar, their physical properties are subpar."

"What do you mean?" Annie asks.

"They can't match the texture, mouthfeel, and appearance that sugar gives to pastries," Julie says.

A mischievous smile plays on Gabriel's lips. "Is this your way of preparing us for a foul taste?"

"The taste is decent, if I do say so myself," Julie claims.

"What I want you to do is rate the various aspects of this lemon mille-feuille on a scale of one to ten in all objectivity."

She passes the tray around, and everybody picks up a mini mille-feuille served on a mini napkin.

Rose studies the delicately layered creation. "Smells lovely. Looks good, too. What sweetener did you use this time?"

"A combination I've been testing this month," Julie says. "Sorry, can't reveal more—trade secret."

Rose pops the test morsel into her mouth. Its tangy custard is perfect... The thin paste tastes and feels right... The overall flavor works well... Curious if there's going to be a funny aftertaste caused by stevia, like in Julie's previous experiment, Rose holds out before rendering her verdict.

Gabriel's admiring gaze meets Julie's. "This one is amazing, babe!"

Her cheeks turn a soft pink at his compliment. "Flattery will get you everywhere, Capitaine Adinian!"

"I'll say that this is your best experimental mille-feuille yet," Flo declares. "Eight out of ten."

When no aftertaste kicks in, Rose feels free to pronounce herself. "I believe you got it just right this time, darling! Nine from me."

"Ten," Annie says before shifting her eyes to Rose. "Can we talk about the case now, please?"

# CHAPTER 22

*J*ulie clears the napkins and brews some tea, while Rose updates Julie, Flo, and Gabriel on everything she's dug up so far with Annie's active help.

When she's done, Annie flattens both hands on the table. "We must call the Chantomes."

"To relay what you learned from Big Napo?" Julie asks.

"Jacques and Monique need to know that René had been kidnapped and ransomed three months before his death," Annie says. "I'm sure they'd been told the same belly-wash as I was when René turned up at home with bruises and a swollen face."

Rose nods. "They need to know the truth about their father, too."

"Isn't it better to let them keep their illusions?" Flo asks. "The incident was unrelated to René's death. Is it really a good idea to cause Jacques and Monique unnecessary disappointment in their late father?"

Annie stares at her, clearly flabbergasted.

"You post-truth kids!" Rose tut-tuts at Flo. "Setting the

record straight is always a good idea, even if it causes someone disappointment or offense."

Flo seems to mull over Rose's words. "I'm all for speaking the truth, Grandma. It's just that in these particular circumstances it might do more harm than good."

"See? You just confirmed my statement." Rose shoots her a teasing smile. "Annie and I grew up in a world where the truth was at the top of the value ladder. Now it's somewhere in the middle."

Recovering from her torpor, Annie says, "We should tell the Chantomes about Pierre-François even from the post-truth standpoint."

"How so?" Flo asks.

"During our dinner in Le Crotoy, Jacques called René a fraud," Annie says.

Rose nods in support, "He dropped enough hints to make it clear he didn't hold René in high esteem."

"He probably believes René had really murdered his roommate Grégoire," Gabriel offers.

"No doubt," Annie agrees. "But ask yourself, why would he believe that his brother committed such a heinous crime? Because he thinks he knows something, and that thing makes René a bad person."

"Jacques must've seen or overheard something," Rose picks up. "He figured out the Mob had kidnapped René, but he drew the wrong conclusions. Jacques blames René for the misdeeds of their father."

Flo points at her with an open palm. "Ah, now I get it!"

"Are you going to call them?" Rose asks Annie.

"I believe this deserves a face-to-face," Annie says. "I'll travel back to Le Crotoy as soon as my knees permit a long trip like that."

Gabriel raises a finger. "My turn now."

Rose clutches the sides of her seat. Gabriel was supposed

to look at the testimonies in René's file for the credible witnesses who had invented René's infatuation with Bernadette. Whoever they were, those liars might very well be Grégoire's and René's murderers.

"I have some disappointing news, I'm afraid," Gabriel says. "The pages with those particular testimonies are missing along with the full list of witnesses."

"You mean they weren't included in your copy of the file?" Julie asks. "A clerical mistake?"

Gabriel's mouth paints a regretful smile. "That's what I'd hoped. But then I checked with the archive. Those pages are missing from the original dossier, too."

"Someone destroyed them!" Rose cries out.

Julie slants a look at Gabriel. "There must've been an insider who had access to the file."

"If this were a recent case, I would've requested an internal investigation," Gabriel says. "But it's too late now."

Annie clenches her fists. "I'm so angry! René was going to be indicted based on fake testimonies, and now we can't even see who was behind them!"

"Something tells me that looking into the lead investigator might yield a clue," Julie says, casting Gabriel a questioning glance. "Do you have a name?"

Gabriel pulls a small notebook from his pocket. "Richard Frinnier. I checked his file and saw nothing to suggest he was crooked."

"Doesn't mean he wasn't," Julie points out.

"I agree. I suggest you look into him," Rose says to Julie, always happy to delegate Internet research.

"No problem!" Julie turns to Gabriel. "By the way, how was Grégoire murdered?"

"He was strangled in his sleep with a belt or a tie," Gabriel replies. "The police didn't find it."

"Fingerprints?" Flo asks.

Gabriel shakes his head. "Not on the body."

Flo knits her eyebrows. "Does that mean that all the evidence pointing at René was circumstantial?"

"Yes," Gabriel says. "That said, René didn't have an alibi for the night of Grégoire's murder, and he was inside the apartment."

"How did the police establish that?" Flo asks.

"René told them," Gabriel replies. "He said he was alone in his room, asleep. Assuming someone else killed Grégoire, René should've heard that person come in. But he told the investigators he'd slept like a log."

Julie rubs her chin. "Were there any signs of struggle in Grégoire's room? Any defensive wounds on his body?"

"None."

"René had the means, a motive, and an opportunity," Rose sums up. "And since he was Grégoire's friend, it's understandable that Grégoire didn't expect to be attacked by him."

"You're not helping," Annie hisses at her.

"No, but I'm putting myself into Frinnier's shoes," Rose says. "It's important to understand why the police made René their prime suspect."

Annie doesn't seem happy with Rose's reply. "What about all the weirdness around the revived PRAC?" she asks. "Should we look into that?"

"You mean Elinor Hugonet's accidental death and the things her boyfriend said at the fete?" Leaning back, Rose crosses her legs. "I believe it's a promising lead."

Flo smiles indulgently to show she isn't convinced. "It might be a waste of time, looking for connections where there are none."

"Fair enough." Rose turns to Julie and Gabriel. "What do you think? Yay or nay?"

"I can see how tempting it's to imagine that Elinor's death

wasn't an accident and that it's somehow linked to René's," Gabriel begins. "But it's a stretch."

"We could follow up quickly, resisting the allure of rabbit holes and conspiracy theories," Julie suggests.

"Agreed," Annie says. "Rose will talk to Lionel about Elinor Hugonet, Gabriel will take a look at her autopsy report, and if those yield nothing, we won't spend more time on it."

Rose turns to Gabriel. "Do you think you can gain access to Elinor's autopsy report?"

"I'll have to find a way," Gabriel exhales with theatrical resignation. "Otherwise, Medz Mama will use her cane on me."

Rose doesn't doubt he's joking, but she can't help admonishing Annie, "For your information, corporal punishment is illegal nowadays and so is assaulting a gendarme."

"This gendarme"—Annie points an accusatory finger at Gabriel—"taught me how to assault him over multiple sessions. I didn't want to, I swear, but when that mule puts his mind to something, there's no talking sense into him!"

# CHAPTER 23

*R*ose squints at the ancient desktop computer in her cramped home office, her fingers pecking at the keys. She's knee-deep in reviewing a module about surveillance techniques. The material is difficult. She's stressed. And her motivation is far from where she needs it to be.

Lady snores softly at her feet.

"At least someone is relaxed," Rose grumbles.

She has an exam in early January, but she fears she might not pass it. It's December 23. Cat is due to arrive by train tonight with her boyfriend Zack. This will be the first time Rose will meet him, and she's very excited.

Tomorrow, her oldest granddaughter, Vero, flies in from Canada with her daughter Rania. Rose hasn't seen them since last summer. She wants to spend as much time as possible with them, especially with Rania—her only great-grandchild so far. Rania grows so fast! Much too fast.

Reluctantly, Rose refocuses on her module.

"Who knew there were so many laws about surveillance?" she mutters to herself, scrolling through pages of legal jargon.

Lady snorts and moves her legs like she's running. She must be hunting something in her dream.

"You don't have a PI license, but you sniff out a treat like a pro, huh, *louloute*?" Rose whispers before returning her attention to the text on the screen.

But the distractions are too strong. No amount of willpower can make her brain register what she's reading.

*All right, let's take an honest look at this.*

There are two options regarding this course. One is to request an additional year, hoping that it will be granted. The other is to go ahead and fail the exam. Because, between the holidays, family, the ongoing investigation and all the other engagements of hers, Rose has no mental space or energy left. And there is no way she's putting her future career above her family. You might do that sort of thing when you're young, but once you turn sixty-five—and remain sixty-five for the next eleven years—nothing beats family.

*Absolutely, freaking nothing.*

Without giving herself time to reconsider, Rose composes an email to the school administration. The moment she hits Send, she feels liberated. Her shackles are gone! She's her own woman once again. The career of a licensed and compensated PI is still in the pipeline, just not for next year.

Rose checks the time. Cat and Zack won't be here for the next five to six hours. Since that interval is suddenly hers to use as she pleases, why not try to figure out Lionel's family name and give him a call?

Rose's first impulse is to delegate the task to her granddaughter Flo, a digital native. But Flo has a life. As does Julie. And, frankly, if Rose is serious about the whole PI thing, she shouldn't count on Julie and Flo to do the boring work.

She opens a search engine. After a good deal of fumbling, she manages to run a search for the combination of "Lionel" and "PRAC." No results. PRAC's membership isn't public.

And, unfortunately, Lionel doesn't seem to hold any official position within the party. His first name doesn't appear on the organizational chart, or anywhere on the PRAC's website.

*What if I search for Elinor Hugonet instead?*

Quickly, she finds Elinor's Facebook account. Inactive since her death in the summer, it's still accessible. Elinor posted a mix of private and professional stuff, photos and random thoughts. She had a bunch of enthusiastic posts throughout the last year and early this year about the revival of PRAC. She was super excited that her friend Mikel was breathing new life into the party founded by their grandfathers.

Funnily, those posts dry up in the spring of this year.

Rose scrolls through Elinor's photo albums. In some of the pictures, Elinor is with Lionel. Infuriatingly, his last name is never mentioned, and he's never tagged. Rose is so proud she knows about social media tags that it breaks her heart she can't benefit from that knowledge in this case.

*Why wouldn't Elinor tag her boyfriend?*

She tagged other people, all right, so she clearly knew how to do it. Perhaps Lionel is one of those rare young people who aren't on social media. Yes, that must be it.

Well, at least Rose has a few photos of him now. She can crop them to remove Elinor and then run a reverse image search. Which is scary. For the life of her, Rose can't remember how to do it.

*I need a tutorial!*

According to Flo, the Internet has tutorials on everything under the sun. Rose makes a note to find a tutorial on reverse image search after she's done researching Elinor.

*Moving on.*

Rose shuts the Facebook page and types "Elinor Hugonet" into the search box again. Over the next thirty minutes, she browses through the articles Elinor had penned for various online magazines and websites. A prolific writer, Elinor covered all sorts of topics from politics to movies. She also wrote in all kinds of formats, including features, interviews, recipe pages and restaurant reviews. Elinor was quite a gourmet.

*My kind girl!* A lovely girl. Such a shame she died in that mysterious domestic accident. Hopefully, Gabriel will tell us what it was...

Rose is almost ready to start looking for reverse image search tutorials, when she stumbles upon a personal blog with a beautiful, heartrending eulogy for Elinor Hugonet. It's Lionel's blog. The eulogy is signed, "Lionel Regis, forever yours."

Her hands shaking with a mixture of nerves and excitement, Rose inputs "Lionel Regis" into the White Pages phone directory.

*Ta-da!* His number is listed.

Rose picks up the phone and keys in Lionel's number.

The phone rings, and then a male voice says, "*Oui?*"

"*Allô*, is this Lionel Regis?"

"Yes," he replies. "Who's asking?"

"My name is Rose Tassy. I was at the PRAC fete in Paris two weeks ago. The things you said—they stayed with me."

"I'd had too much to drink," Lionel says dryly.

"That may be so, but your words moved me."

"Um... All right."

Rose keeps her voice steady despite the butterflies in her stomach. "I was wondering if we could do a video call with my friend Annie Malian sometime in January to talk about PRAC."

There's a pause at the other end. "May I ask why?"

*I'm going to be as forthcoming as possible.*

"Annie was engaged to a young man who was part of the original PRAC, together with Elinor's and Mikel's grandfathers. He was her first and biggest love. He died in '61."

"O-okay..."

"Annie is eighty-four now, and she's been thinking a lot about René," Rose explains. "It would mean the world to her if she could learn more about that part of his life, including his politics, which she hadn't been aware of at the time."

"Wouldn't Mikel know more than I do about the original PRAC?"

"I talked to him at the fete." Rose makes a split-second decision to add another honest detail. "He was very cautious with his answers."

"Of course, he was," Lionel mutters under his breath.

*Phew! I made the right call.*

"You're a southerner, right?" Lionel asks her unexpectedly. "I can hear it in your accent."

"Damn," Rose says with feigned disappointment. "I was fooling myself that I sound as smooth as you do."

He chuckles. "Are you in the South right now? And if so, where about?"

"Near Arles. Why?"

"I'm spending Christmas in Martigues," he says. "My parents moved here in search of sunshine last year, after they retired."

"That's only twenty minutes' drive from Beldoc!"

"Actually, I have two hours to kill this afternoon..."

Rose glances at her watch. She can drive to Martigues, talk to Lionel for an hour or even two, and be home in time for Cat's arrival.

"Give me an address, and I'll be there," she says into the phone.

"What about Annie?"

"She'll join us over the phone," Rose suggests. "She's less mobile than I am at the moment."

"How about the Accadémia Caffé along The Bird Mirror?"

"I'll be there in half an hour, and I'm buying the drinks!"

# CHAPTER 24

*R*ose steps into the Accadémia Caffé bathed in a beautiful midafternoon light. She spots Lionel immediately, a solitary figure by the window. As she approaches, he looks up, his expression guarded but polite.

He stands to acknowledge her arrival. "Madame Tassy."

"Please, call me Rose," she responds as she takes the seat across from him.

The café hums around them, the clinking of cups and the murmur of conversations forming a backdrop to their improvised meeting. As they wait for the server to approach, Rose dials Annie, but her phone is turned off, same as half an hour ago. She must be napping. Rose leaves her a message to call back as soon as she can.

All the while, Lionel studies Rose. His curiosity is palpable.

Unnerved due to Annie's unavailability, Rose has a difficult time starting the conversation. She focuses on the picturesque view of the Bird Mirror wharf instead. Its water reflects the colorful waterfront buildings like a supersized, shimmery mirror.

She gestures to it through the glass. "The *mirror* part of the name is self-evident, but I don't see any birds…"

"In spring and summer, they nest on the roof of this very café." Lionel points upward. "Then you can see their reflection in the water."

"How very poetic!" Rose exclaims, her eyes meeting Lionel's.

A server shows up and takes their orders.

When he moves on to the next table, Rose decides to go all in. "At the fete, you spoke of puppet masters who own politicians."

"I did."

"You questioned Mikel's probity."

"No, you misunderstood that part," Lionel says. "I questioned if he'd be able to retain it when push comes to shove."

Rose cocks her head. "You mean when Blaise Gimbert comes to collect dividends on his investment?"

Drawing back, Lionel scrutinizes Rose. "How did you find out about that?"

"Like I said, I'm helping my friend Annie learn as much as she can about René's last days and weeks. In doing so, we found out about Blaise's donations and that his father, Joel, provided the funds to kickstart the original PRAC."

"I'm impressed."

It's Rose's turn to peer at him. "But not surprised?"

"No, I'd heard both those juicy tidbits from Elinor."

"Who did Elinor hear them from?"

"Her paternal grandfather," Lionel says.

"Dany Hugonet? Do tell!"

Lionel seems happy to oblige. "Dany had always been tight mouthed about PRAC despite Elie's many attempts to interview him."

"Why did she want to interview him?"

"She wrote lifestyle and culinary columns mainly, but she was dipping a toe into political journalism," Lionel explains. "It was her true passion, what she wanted to do."

"Do you think she was writing an article about PRAC?"

"I know she was," he says. "She'd done a lot of research and had a draft for a feature. It drove her nuts that her own beloved grandpa, the cofounder of PRAC, refused to talk to her about it."

"I'd be mad, too."

"And then last spring... on his deathbed when it wouldn't've occurred to Elie to ask him about PRAC, he started talking."

Lionel falls silent while the server sets their drinks on the table.

Rose leans closer. "Did Dany tell her about a certain René Chantome?"

"Not to my knowledge."

*Damn!* "What did he say to Elinor?"

"He told her about Gimbert's secret money, which Dany had refused before Etienne reversed that decision. Etienne's argument was that PRAC's goals were so noble, they were worth a small compromise."

Rose's mouth twists. "By all means necessary."

"Exactly," Lionel says. "Dany told Elinor it had been a fatal mistake. Those were the last words he choked out before his heart stopped."

"Was that all?" Rose asks.

Lionel hesitates. "Well, when Elie relayed it to me on the day he died, I had the impression it wasn't."

"What gave you that impression?"

"Honestly, I don't know anymore." He lifts his hands and lets them fall. "I just had a sense Dany spoke to her about something else, something important, but she wasn't ready to talk about it yet. Like, she needed time to process that bit."

Rose shuts her eyes in frustration. "Ah, how I wish she'd told you!"

"Me too."

"What about that article you mentioned?" Rose asks. "Have you read it?"

"She'd shown me an early draft in which she talked about the PRAC leadership, including Dany, in glowing terms. She'd written it before his deathbed revelations."

"Do you think she amended the article afterward?"

"I don't know."

"Do you think you could find out? There might be a printout in a desk drawer somewhere." Rose talks as fast as the gears turning in her head. "Did you live together? Are you still in the same apartment?"

"We did, and I am, and I recently worked up the nerve to go through her stuff."

Rose stares at him intently. "And?"

"Well, first, she was comfortable working on a screen, so she hardly printed out anything. Second, I couldn't find her laptop."

Rose knits her eyebrows. "That's weird, isn't it?"

"She might've left it at her parents' place. They live in Paris, too, and she'd visit them once or twice a week." He smiles. "Only child, like me."

"Have you asked them about the laptop?"

He shakes his head. "They're still devastated, crushed. Every time we talk, it ends with them weeping their hearts out."

One of the many boring topics covered in her PI program comes to Rose's mind.

"What about backups?" she asks Lionel. "You know that Internet drawer where people store their files?"

"You mean the cloud?"

"Yes! She might have put her revised article on the cloud."

"If she did, I don't have access to it," Lionel says. "Elie and I respected each other's privacy. We didn't share passwords and such."

Desperately, Rose tries to recall what she's learned in her course about how family members of a deceased person could access those digital files. Unfortunately, she can't remember anything conclusive. And, regardless, given that Lionel and Elinor weren't married, he wouldn't qualify.

*Elinor's parents, on the other hand...*

Lionel finishes his drink. "I'm afraid I must go now, Madame Tassy. I'm sorry if I couldn't be more helpful."

He moves to call the server, but Rose swats his hand. "I said the drinks are on me!"

The server acknowledges her from across the room, takes a step, stumbles on something, and falls face down. A bunch of customers surround him at once and help him up as he rubs his forehead. Which reminds Rose she nearly forgot to ask an important question.

She turns to Lionel. "If I may, what exactly happened to Elinor? Did she fall and hit her head? Did she get electrocuted?"

"She breathed in too much cinnamon powder," Lionel says.

Rose stares at him, unsure she heard him right.

A sad little smile quirks Lionel's lips. "I get that reaction a lot. You see, ground cinnamon can kill you if you inhale more than your lungs can absorb."

"What quantities are we talking about?"

"In Elie's case, a small jar."

Rose blinks, even more confused. "Why would she breathe in a jar of ground cinnamon?"

"She didn't inhale all of it and not on purpose, obviously."

Rose searches his face. "Can you tell me what happened?"

"I was at work. Elie was alone at home, testing a new recipe for cinnamon buns for her food column. A jar of ground cinnamon slipped from her grasp. The worktops in our kitchen are granite and high. Elie was petite." His voice cracks.

The server wobbles past their table. "I'll be back with your check in a moment."

"Take your time," Rose tells him. "Be sure to apply some ice to that bump on your forehead!"

"The jar broke," Lionel carries on. "A cloud of cinnamon dust burst into Elie's face. The ME believes she lost her balance before she could step away, so she breathed in quite a bit. Too much for someone with asthma."

Instinctively, Rose places her palm at the base of her throat. "Did she... choke on it and die?"

"Cinnamon is made up of cellulose, which our body can't handle in large amounts," Lionel says. "If you aspirate too much, it gets trapped in your airways, which leads to an inflammatory response. Ground cinnamon is so fine, it can get very deep into your lungs, and if it forms a clump that blocks your—"

He pauses again and averts his gaze, too upset to continue.

Rose's heart goes out to him. Anyone's would, no doubt. And having lost her only daughter, her precious Elise, to a tragic accident, Rose knows all too well what Lionel went through. You make plans for the weekend, worry about little things, and suddenly, there's glaring void in your life. You're overwhelmed by the crushing injustice of it. All you feel is rage, helplessness, and bottomless sorrow. On a loop.

When Lionel looks at her again, his black eyes glisten. "I'm giving you all that science because I can't bear the image that the short reply paints in my mind. She choked and died before she could call for help."

ANA T. DREW

The server arrives with the check. In silence, Rose pays and they walk out of the café.

"I'm glad I agreed to talk to you," Lionel says.

"You are?"

"At first, I worried it would be like rubbing salt into my wound. And it was, but..." He gazes at the wharf.

"What?"

"It was also therapeutic," he says, turning to Rose.

"I'm happy to hear that!" She hands him her business card. "Call me if you remember anything new."

"Will do."

They say their goodbyes, and Rose hops into her car.

All she can think of on her drive back home is how innocuous Elinor's "killer" turned out to be and how fragile the human body is.

Once at home, with an hour left until Cat's arrival, she takes Lady for a walk. While the pup checks her pee mail along Sarah's hedge, Rose sends a text to everyone in her contacts warning them to keep their ground cinnamon in containers that are shatterproof.

160

# CHAPTER 25

The door swings open, and in walks Cat, her cheeks flushed from the cold, followed by a tall, fair-haired, bespectacled man.

"Grandma, this is Zack," Cat introduces him.

After the customary greetings and Lady's dance of joy around Cat, Rose leads them to the kitchen. The table is set for three, and Rose has made Cat's favorite onion quiche.

"Are you in the same line of work as Cat?" Rose asks Zack while they eat.

"I'm a cryptographer," Zack says.

"I thought so! Did you meet through work or a professional association?"

Zack does a double take before glancing at Cat.

"Cryptography is a field of mathematics, Grandma," Cat says with a chuckle. "Zack works with codes and algorithms, not spirits."

Rose stares at him. "Is that true?"

"Clearly, I don't look like a mathematician to you," he says.

"No, no, you do," Rose assures him. "My surprise was directed at myself."

"What do you mean?"

Rose pouts. "I've sixty-five years of age believing that cryptography is the study of cryptic writings."

Cat stifles a giggle.

Zack gives Rose an earnest smile. "I see why you'd think that, Rose. Oceanographers study the oceans. There is no reason why cryptographers should do math instead of studying cryptic writings."

*It's settled—I like this boy.*

After dinner, Cat and Zack volunteer to take Lady for her final walk of the day.

Rose checks her phone. She missed a call from Annie! Settling into her favorite armchair, she calls back.

"You tried to reach me this afternoon," Annie says.

"Yes."

"And then you texted me about how to store ground cinnamon."

"I did."

"But you didn't pick up when I called back," Annie says. "So, I'm very confused."

"My Parisian granddaughter arrived with her boyfriend, so I didn't hear your call," Rose explains, and then goes on to recount her meeting with Lionel.

Annie listens without interruption.

"How embarrassing!" she exclaims when Rose finishes. "I take naps while you do all the leg work."

"You hired me to do it."

"You're doing it free of charge," Annie points out. "I don't think the term 'hire' applies in our case."

"You may be right."

Annie lets out a long, loud sigh. "I'm beginning to give up on the idea of telling Jacques and Monique the truth about their father in person. It doesn't look like I'll be able to travel to Le Crotoy anytime soon."

"Video calls aren't so bad, you know?"

"Yes, they are." Annie exhales again. "I wish the Chantomes would come here, so we could talk face-to-face without waiting until I can walk again!"

"Invite them, then."

"What will I say to them? 'Hey, I have some info for you, but if want to hear it, you must travel all the way to my house,' That's too cheeky."

"At least as far as Lionel is concerned, I don't see what benefit your presence would've added," Rose offers by way of a comfort.

But once the words are out, she realizes that Annie will probably misinterpret them as Rose's way of telling her she's useless. "I didn't mean—" she begins.

Annie interrupts her, "I'm aware you meant well, don't worry. We've been talking daily over the past three weeks, so I'm beginning to know you."

"Oh. Good."

Annie pants, like someone experiencing sharp pain.

"Are you all right?" Rose asks, panicking. "Was that your knee?"

"No, it was my head."

"*Merde*! Are you in your room? Can you shout for help?"

"Stop fretting," Annie says with a laugh. "I gasped because I recalled something from our meeting with Blaise Gimbert."

"What?"

"At one point he said to your reporter friend... What was his name?"

"Noam," Rose prompts.

"Right. He said that Noam wasn't the first journalist who

found out about his sponsorship of PRAC and thought they held something big."

"Yes, I remember it!" Rose's imagination takes it from there. "What if... What if Elinor had finished her article and contacted Blaise with a request for comment?"

"It's possible."

"And what if he got spooked? He told us he didn't care if the word got out, but what if it was a lie?"

"Equally possible."

Rose switches hands and puts the phone to her other ear. "What if Elinor's death wasn't an accident?"

Annie begins to protest, but Rose shushes her, "Hear me out. Blaise could've sent a hitman to sneak into Elinor's home, restrain her, blow cinnamon in her face, wait until she choked to death, and sneak out with her laptop?"

"That's the most far-fetched theory I've ever heard."

"Why?" Rose bristles. "It's very clever if you think about it. No one doubts that Elinor's death was a tragic accident because cinnamon as a murder weapon is too 'far-fetched,' as you said. And it explains the missing laptop!"

"She was baking, Rose. How could the hitman know that? How could they know she'd be testing a cinnamon bun recipe for her column that afternoon? And she didn't fight him. Why wouldn't she fight someone restraining her?"

"How do you know she didn't fight? Has Gabriel seen the autopsy report?"

"No," Annie says. "I used the deduction method."

"Care to elaborate?"

"If Elinor had fought your hitman, there would've been bruises or other signs of struggle on her body. The police wouldn't have ruled her death accidental."

*Annie's deduction is solid; there's no denying it.* "Yes, well, perhaps I'm wrong on this."

"Not every death is a murder, my dear."

Rose snorts. "Says the woman who spent sixty-odd years believing her fiancé's suicide was murder!"

"That's different," Annie murmurs.

Rose's vexation falls as quickly as it rose.

Over the next few minutes, they wrap up the call and wish each other a merry Christmas. Annie's family will be celebrating it twice—tomorrow with the rest of the country and then again in January with the Orthodox world.

After they hang up, Rose makes another call, to the hotel Les Tonneaux.

It's Jacques' daughter Hélène who picks up. Rose asks for Monique.

"We uncovered some information that you and Jacques need to know," Rose says to Monique.

"What is it?"

"It's up to Annie to tell you."

"Pass her the phone, then," Monique says.

"She's not with me now; she's stuck at home."

"Stuck?"

"Her knees are acting up," Rose explains.

There's a brief silence, during which Rose decides to put on a bold front. It's always easier to be brazen on somebody else's behalf.

"Would you consider coming down to Provence after Christmas?" she asks.

"Why not?" Monique replies to her delight. "I always liked Annie. Now that I know she was in love with René, I like her even more."

"What about Jacques?"

"I doubt he'll budge."

"Even if you tell him the news will blow his mind?" Rose asks.

"I can't tell him anything because we haven't spoken in sixty years."

"But you communicate through Hélène," Rose points out. "I saw you do it during the post-quiz dinner."

There's some shifting and sighing on the other end, and then Monique says, "I suppose I can ask Hélène to relay your message. It might help if you give me something more specific."

"Have Hélène tell him that his suspicions were correct, to a degree."

"Really?"

"The Mob took René," Rose says. "Pierre-François sold everything to ransom him. But René had never had any 'shady dealings' with Le Milieu."

Monique is silent for a moment, probably digesting what she just heard.

Finally, she asks, "If René had been innocent, then why the secrecy? Why couldn't Papa tell us, his family, what was going on?"

"Come down to the South with Jacques, and all your questions will be answered!"

# CHAPTER 26

*R*ose puts a footstool next to the Christmas tree, its branches still bare and waiting. The rest of the decorations are up. Twinkling lights strung around the windows cast a warm glow on the furniture, people, plants, and animals present in the room. Well, one animal.

Lady is sniffing around the coffee table, no doubt plotting to steal a cookie.

Vero, Rose's oldest granddaughter, is talking with Gabriel and Zack. Vero and Rania flew in just in time for Christmas Eve dinner. Vero's husband stayed back in Montreal to spend the holidays with his aging parents.

The other notable absence this year is Laurent. Rose's son-in-law was held up in Paris by some work emergency. After Elise died nearly twenty years ago, the relationship between Rose and Laurent was strained. But then he showed up last Christmas. And, somehow, they were able to rebuild the bridges they'd burned over the years.

Karl and his dog Harley were invited, but Karl declined. He told Rose they'd already accepted another invitation. He didn't specify from who.

On the plus side, all of Rose's girls are present, along with three boyfriends—Julie's Gabriel, Flo's Tino and Cat's Zack. Rose feels like she's the luckiest woman alive. And a damn resilient bugger, too!

*Life is full of surprises, isn't it?*

When Elise died, Rose's world went dark. She carried on for her granddaughters' sakes, but she sincerely didn't expect to ever experience joy again. How could she when nothing she saw, heard, or felt—no sensory or intellectual input whatsoever—could bypass the filter of her comfortless loss?

*And look at me now!*

Rose climbs on the footstool. "Hey, Rania, I'm in position. Ready to work your magic on the tree?"

Rania, usually the tree-decorating enthusiast, barely lifts her eyes from her phone. "In a minute, Granny!"

"Come on, lazy pants, let's get this tree decorated," Rose insists.

Sighing, Rania puts her phone down. "Okay, but only if we can listen to some cool Christmas remixes."

Rose agrees. Rania pairs her phone with the speaker Flo gave Rose last Christmas, and soon the room is filled with a very modern version of "Jingle Bells."

"It's hip-hop," Rania says.

Rose points to the cardboard box on the floor. "Pass me the star, will you?"

"Do you like hip-hop, Granny?" Rania asks, handing her the ornament.

"I prefer the original."

Rania mumbles something, disappointed. They continue hanging baubles and wrapping the tree in strings of lights for a while.

Meanwhile, Cat fastens a small Santa hat on Lady's head.

"Isn't she adorable?" She turns to Rose. "Do you think she'll wear it?"

"Not if she values her dignity," Rania says.

Cat shakes her head. "Aren't you too young for the attitude?"

"That wasn't attitude," Vero replies for her daughter. "That was just snark."

Cat hikes an eyebrow. "What's attitude then?"

"Attitude is when I ask her to do something, and she says, 'Why?' And I say, 'Because I birthed and nurtured you,' and she says, 'I never asked you to.'"

"That means she's real," Rose concludes.

To multiple puzzled looks, she clarifies, "If your preteen has never told you she didn't ask to be born, then she's a product of your overactive imagination."

"Thank you, Madame Freud!" Vero gives Rose a hug.

Once the Christmas tree is decorated and the gift boxes piled underneath, Rose herds everyone to the coffee table for the predinner *apéritif*. Lady abandons her plan to snatch a cookie and curls up by the fireplace. Her Santa hat is still on.

Rose raises her glass. "To you, my darlings, and to the joy of Christmas! Thank you for being here with me!"

Glasses clink. Toasts are made to Rose, to family, to Christmas. Rose feels a soft hand slip into hers.

"Never mind my snark, OK?" Rania whispers. "I love you, Granny."

Rose's eyes well up. "I love you more."

Given how much she loathes getting emotional in public, she lets go of Rania's hand at once and turns to Gabriel. "Did you manage to lay your hands on Elinor's autopsy report? Any chance her death was murder?"

Out of the corner of her eye, she notices Zack shoot a bewildered glance at Cat.

"I told you my folks were weird," Cat says to her boyfriend. "But then, mediums rarely grow up in normie families."

Gabriel gives Rose a crooked smile. "I haven't seen the autopsy report yet, but I can tell you that Commissaire Zaoui, who was in charge of her case, was very thorough. For example, he checked if Lionel Regis was indeed at work at the time of her death."

Rose frowns. "Why would he do that?"

"Because when a healthy young woman dies, her intimate partner is always a person of interest," Gabriel says. "One-third of all female victims of murder were killed by their partner."

Rose chews on her bottom lip. "Was Lionel at work, like he claimed?"

"He was."

*Phew*. Rose realizes just how much sympathy she has developed for Lionel over their brief acquaintance. If it turned out he was guilty, she might lose faith in humanity.

"Zaoui also followed up on something Lionel had mentioned during his interview," Gabriel continues.

"What?" Rose, Julie, and Flo ask at the same time.

"A few days before her death, Lionel had caught Elinore having words with Mikel Poupon after a gathering at PRAC's Parisian headquarters. When Lionel got nearer, they stopped arguing. Elinor wouldn't tell him what it was about."

Rose stares at Gabriel. "I had a long conversation with Lionel yesterday afternoon, and he never mentioned it."

"Maybe because Zaoui had confirmed Mikel's alibi," Gabriel suggests. "I imagine Lionel didn't want to speak disloyally, again, of someone who had been checked and cleared."

"How good was Mikel's alibi?" Julie asks.

"Ironclad," Gabriel replies. "He wasn't in Paris."

Rose makes a face. "He could be lying."

"There's plenty of proof, including videos of the talk he

was giving to young activists in Nantes when Elinor died," Gabriel counters.

Rose peers at him. "So, both Lionel and Mikel had an alibi. Was there anyone else in their circle who didn't have one?"

"Mikel's wife, Katia," Gabriel says. "A neighbor heard a woman shouting in Elinor's apartment around noon, which is when she died."

Julie leans forward. "Shouting what?"

"The neighbor couldn't make it out."

"How do we know it was Katia?" Rose asks.

"Zaoui checked the CCTV footage from cameras on Elinor's street. He spotted Katia Poupon going in and then leaving Elinor's building."

Rose clamps a hand to her mouth. *Did Katia kill Elinor by blowing cinnamon in her face?* But then why isn't she behind bars?

Gabriel breaks the suspenseful silence. "Here's the thing. Katia left the building at ten thirty-five. Elinor choked and died at half past noon, two hours later. Katia couldn't have killed her. The neighbor had gotten the time wrong."

Vero looks from him to Rose. "Sounds like Elinor's death was an accident."

"Yes," Gabriel confirms. "I just wanted you to know that the police did their job and checked everyone who could have had a motive or opportunity to get rid of Elinor."

"Why did Katia go to see Elinor?" Julie asks.

"They were close friends, and they lived in the same neighborhood," Gabriel says. "They dropped by each other's place all the time. She told Zaoui they had discussed a rally that PRAC was co-organizing with other parties."

Julie rubs her chin. "But why the shouting? Didn't you say the neighbor heard Katia shout?"

"Maybe Katia wasn't actually shouting," Gabriel says.

"Maybe she merely raised her voice in excitement, and the neighbor made a mistake just like with the time of her visit."

"But we do know from Lionel that Mikel and Elinor had argued." Flo shifts her eyes to Rose. "You talked with Lionel. Do you have an idea what the argument could've been about?"

"Her article," Rose says. "I'll bet money on it." She goes on to tell them about Dany Hugonet's deathbed confession and how Elinor was writing a feature for her paper about PRAC. She had probably revised it to include the info about Joel Gimbert funding Etienne Poupon's creation back in the fifties and sixties, and his son Blaise pulling the same number with Mikel Poupon's new edition.

All while she talks, she can't stop thinking that Blaise must've had something to do with Elinor's accidental death. She doesn't dare say it aloud, expecting the same counterarguments that Annie gave her. It is a far-fetched theory, no doubt.

But when helping Julie with her cases, Rose had had even wilder theories, some of which turned out to be true.

With still an hour left to the dinner Julie and Vero are preparing, Rose retreats to her home office. She must stop thinking about Blaise Gimbert, or else she won't be much fun tonight. To get him off her mind, there is only one thing she can do.

She fires up her computer and types an email to Blaise Gimbert.

Monsieur Gimbert,

May I share my new theory with you?

In late 1960, René Chantome threatened to expose your

father Joel as PRAC's main source of funding. But then René killed himself, and the problem went away.

Earlier this year, Dany Hugonet told his granddaughter Elinor about it on his deathbed. She put it in her article. Before publishing it in the paper she worked for, she reached out to you for comment.

You hated your father's portrayal in that piece. You also feared that Elinor's article would open the possibility of uncovering your father's implication in the murder of Grégoire Lacaze and René Chantome.

And so, you ordered her silenced for good, just like your father had done with René.

Change my mind.

Sincerely,
Rose Tassy

# CHAPTER 27

*A*nnie gets off the bus that brought her to Beldoc and hails a cab. This is her first big outing after the latest arthritic flare-up in her knees kept her minimally mobile for almost a month. She's taking it easy.

The investigation was on pause so that Annie and Rose could spend every waking hour with their families. It's January 3 today, which means that the Catholic Christmas and New Year are behind Annie. The Armenian Orthodox Christmas will be celebrated on January 6, thus completing Annie's trifecta of winter's festive events.

Over the last week, there was much cooking, feasting, doing the dishes, talking, arguing, laughing, drunken singing, and dancing. The latter had Annie cheering from the spectator seat. Even as her knees got better, she knew that her dancing days were over.

The taxi driver delivers her to Rose's gate and helps her out. She tips him generously. Stepping carefully, she crosses the garden to the entrance and rings the doorbell.

Rose greets her with a hug. "Happy New Year, darling!"

"Happy New Year!" Surprised at the outburst, but pleased, Annie taps Rose's back. "It's good to see you."

The dog clamors for attention, so Annie pets her. Satisfied, Lady wags her tail and trots across the entryway. Rose follows her. Annie follows Rose.

In Rose's gorgeous verandah, Annie lifts her face to the sunlight that streams in from all directions. The last time she was here, this space was arranged for the doga class. The wicker furniture was pushed aside, and yoga mats were everywhere. Now, the sofas, coffee table and armchairs are where they're supposed to be.

In a corner surrounded by sprawling plants, Rose has set a table with a thermal insulated kettle, cups, and pastries. She guides Annie to a comfy armchair and helps her into it before sitting down. Lady stretches out in a patch of sunlight at their feet.

Annie can smell cardamom as Rose pours fragrant tea into delicate porcelain cups.

"Julie made this Christmas blend for me," Rose says.

Annie breathes in deeply, savoring the aroma. "Ah, this is just what my soul needed!"

"Did you enjoy the holidays?" Rose inquires.

"Baby Max kept us laughing," Annie replies. "But let us talk about the case. You said on the phone that Blaise Gimbert replied to your email."

"Not him personally, but his lawyer." Rose picks up her phone and pushes it in front of Annie.

Annie stares at the unintelligible text. "I'm going to need a magnifying glass for this."

To her surprise, Rose has one in a little drawer under the table. Annie holds it to the screen and reads.

Dear Madame Tassy,

175

My client, Monsieur Gimbert, communicated to you during your in-person interview that he is not concerned if his support for the revived Party of Radical Anti-Capitalists becomes publicly known. This has not changed. He believes that in the current political climate, individuals of substantial wealth who finance socially progressive causes can do so in an undisguised manner.

Furthermore, Monsieur Gimbert asserted that his late father would never have employed an extreme and illicit measure such as an assassination, regardless of his desire to maintain confidentiality concerning his financial support of the original PRAC. The very notion of such an act is inconceivable and contrary to the principles upheld by the Gimbert family.

Rose scrolls down.

"Wait! Go back," Annie asks her. "I need to read that again to be sure I understood what he's trying to say."

"He's just rehashing in legalese what Blaise told us during the interview."

Annie squints at Rose. "He doesn't mind the publicity for his funding of PRAC and his dad was too good to order a hit job. Right?"

"Exactly." Rose scrolls down to the next section of the letter.

Secondly, Elinor Hugonet never solicited a statement from Monsieur Gimbert in reference to an inflammatory article depicting Monsieur Joel Gimbert in a negative light. Had she sought such a response, there is little doubt that it would have been declined. Instead, I might have raised the matter with the owner of the newspaper that employs her, a friend of Monsieur Gimbert's.

Furthermore, had she endeavored to submit the piece to another outlet, its acceptance would have been highly improbable. No mainstream media would air or publish her segment. We may have many different media outlets, Madame Tassy, but they are owned by a very small group of like-minded people.

If Madame Hugonet chose to post her article online independently, I would have hired specialized services to make her blog undiscoverable in search engines.

I hope that it is evident from the aforementioned information that Monsieur Gimbert possesses an extensive array of lawful avenues at his disposal. Consequently, if he had wished to make Madame Hugonet's unfavorable article go away, there would have been neither a necessity nor an inclination on his part to engage in any illicit activities.

With kind regards,
Christophe Carron

Annie looks up. "So many words to say that Blaise didn't do it, because he neither wished nor needed to do it."

"That pretty much sums it up."

They spend a few minutes sipping tea and nibbling on pastries.

"What about Katia Poupon?" Annie asks.

"She couldn't have done it. She'd left the building almost two hours before Elinore inhaled cinnamon and died."

"I know that, but shouldn't we call her?"

Rose puckers her face. "Why?"

"To ask what they talked about?"

"She already told Commissaire Zaoui," Rose says. "Some rally they were planning."

"What if she lied?"

"Hmm... Say, she did. Why wouldn't she lie to us, too?"

"She probably will," Annie agrees. "But on the off chance she doesn't, isn't it worth a try?"

Rose taps her finger on the side of her cup. "It's true that when Julie investigates a case, she talks to everyone involved, no matter how useful she expects it to be."

"If we are ever to get to the bottom of this, then we have to do like Julie," Annie says.

Taking her phone from Annie, Rose checks the online phone directory for Katia Poupon. Nothing comes up. She must've opted out. Next, Rose keys in Katia's husband's name, Mikel Poupon. Still nothing.

She calls Lionel and puts him on speaker. "Did you know that Katia visited Elinor the morning she died?"

"I did."

Rose knits her eyebrows. "But you didn't mention it when we talked in Martigues."

"Look, Katia had been gone for two hours when Elinor aspirated the cinnamon, so I didn't want to—"

"Yes, yes, bad-mouth your friends." Rose puffs in frustration. "Listen, Lionel, you can't keep protecting them, and at the same time hoping to learn the truth about Elinor's murder."

Annie grimaces at the last word. *Pushing it too far, my friend.*

"Murder?" Lionel's voice is laced with disbelief. "What are you talking about? It was an accident."

"I'm sure it was," Rose agrees at once.

*What was that all about?* Did Rose try to plant a seed of doubt in Lionel's mind?

After a brief silence, Rose says, "I just wanted to call Katia to see if she knew anything that might help us untangle this knot. I wasn't going to blame her for Elinor's death or anything. But, never mind."

"I'll give you her number," Lionel offers unexpectedly. "Let me know if anything relevant comes up."

"Of course! We're in the same boat," Rose assures him.

After they end the call, Annie can't help but wonder what boat that is, exactly.

Is it the Ferry of the Unconsolably Bereft? Its passengers refuse to believe that their loved one took his own life or died in a pointless domestic accident. They think they can find closure only if they hunt down the evil one responsible for their loss.

Or is it the Canoe of Tenacious Truth Seekers? This bunch can sense when things don't add up, and so they refuse to stop looking until they can figure out why.

*Am I deluding myself or am I right to persevere?*

The self-doubt that had stopped Annie from asking questions for over sixty years is back. And it's hitting her with a vengeance.

# CHAPTER 28

Two minutes and a swig of tea later, Annie glances at Rose. "Ready?"

With a nod, Rose picks up her phone again. "I'm going to bluff."

"Is that a good idea?"

"Do you have a better one?"

Annie shakes her head.

Rose inputs Katia's number.

A woman picks up. "*Allô?*"

"Hello and happy New Year! Is this Katia Poupon?" Rose puts her on speakerphone.

"Yes, who's asking?"

"Rose Tassy. We met at the PRAC fete last month."

"Oh, I remember you!" Katia's voice softens with recognition. "Happy New Year, Rose! What have you been up to?"

"I've helping my friend Annie Malian, who's here with me, to unravel a messy affair that spans decades."

"Sounds exciting."

"Wait until you hear the really exciting bit," Rose says.

"You can help us."

"Me? How?"

Rose shoots Annie a glance before speaking into the phone. "You went to see Elinor the day she died."

Katia seems to have lost her tongue.

Rose plows on, "We believe it was to try and persuade her not to publish her article about PRAC."

"Elinor and I were friends," Katia says after a pause, "but I never interfered with her journalistic choices."

"Except in this case, her choice would've hurt your husband's political career."

The other side of the line goes silent again. Annie looks at Rose. Bluffing like that was a bold thing to do, but what now? Why would Katia admit to anything that makes her and her husband look bad when she knows Rose can't prove it? Elinor is dead, and the neighbor who overheard them couldn't make out what they were talking about.

Finally, Katia responds, "You have no idea how wrong you are, Rose!"

*She's going to tell us they were planning a rally, and that will be that.*

"Elie had big doubts about her article," Katia says. "That morning, when I went to see her, she'd made up her mind to bury that story and move on."

Annie's mouth falls open. *Katia isn't dodging!* Quite the contrary, she's confirming Rose's theory—at least in part.

"Elinor had worked very hard on that piece," Rose says. "It had revelations that could make some waves. I'm not convinced she'd give up on her chance to break into political journalism for the sake of your husband's career."

"She wasn't going to at first."

"You lost me."

A bitter little laugh comes from Katia's end of the line.

"Elie had submitted the article to the editor in chief at her paper. His initial reaction was, 'This is gold!'"

"And then what happened?"

"And then he was told by his boss, the owner of the paper, that the article wasn't going to be published."

While Annie digests that bit, Rose exclaims, "Holy cow, Blaise Gimbert's lawyer wasn't being hypothetical in his email! He had actually had Elinor's editor ax her story."

"Elie was told that no other mainstream paper or magazine would print her piece," Katia says. "Her options were to go to smaller, web-based media or to post it on her own blog."

"And she decided not to?" Rose asks, her voice laced with incredulity.

"She was leaning that way," Katia replies. "What reach would a blog have compared to a national newspaper? Elinor feared she would antagonize Mikel and me for a story no one would ever see."

Annie mutters, "Blaise Gimbert's strategy was working."

"Your husband struck me as a very ambitious man," Rose says into the phone. "He would've resented Elinor's going public, even from a tiny outlet with limited reach."

"He did resent it," Katia says. "But I didn't."

*What?* Annie didn't expect that.

Rose, on the other hand, doesn't seem surprised.

"Funny you'd say that... It reminds me of some strange comments you made at the fete."

Katia smirks. "I'd had too much wine that evening. I was hoping no one had paid attention to my yammer."

"But I was!" Rose says triumphantly. "I noticed your lack of faith in your husband."

"It isn't that I don't have faith in him," Katia protests. "It's just... politics is such a dirty business!"

Rose skews a knowing smile. "It sure is."

"And it takes a toll not only on the person in question, but on their loved ones, too," Katia goes on. "I have a premonition that if Mikel continues on this path, it will destroy our family."

"Not an unfounded fear," Annie chimes in. "Just look at our recent presidents and presidential hopefuls who ended up divorced!"

Rose's eyes widen. "You're helping Mikel, but you resent his political ambition! You don't want him to run for office."

"I never openly admitted it to anyone besides Elie, but you're right, I don't."

Rose's mouth forms an O as if she's had yet another light bulb moment. "That pretty young thing who was all over your husband... er, Louise, does she have something to do with your lack of enthusiasm?"

"He isn't sleeping with her," Katia says quickly. "But she's prettier and younger than me, and he finds her adoration flattering."

"She'll keep trying, won't she?" Rose asks in a quiet, sympathetic voice.

"Like a vulture wheeling over a wounded beast!"

Annie leans closer to the phone. "Did you go to Elinor's to persuade her to publish her article despite her doubts, hoping it would ruin Mikel's political ambitions and save your marriage?"

"Yes," Katia admits.

"Does Mikel know about the advice you gave Elinor?" Rose inquires.

"No, he doesn't," she says. "He didn't even know I'd gone to see her until the police came by asking about it."

Annie has more questions. "You said he wasn't happy about the revelations in Elinor's article. How much did they bother him?"

"Do you mean how far he'd have gone to stop Elie?" Katia asks.

Annie shifts in her seat. "We know he has a rock-solid alibi, so there's that."

"He's a good man, you know?" Katia says. "He tried to talk Elie out of it, sure. But he also told her that if she chose to publish her article, he'd deal with the fallout."

"How noble of him!" Annie exclaims.

"He *is* noble," Katia says.

"And devilishly handsome," Rose adds, as if that were relevant. "One more question, Katia, if I may. Had you seen the final draft of Elinor's article?"

"Yes."

"Did it talk about the Gimberts funding for both the original and revived PRAC?"

"Yes."

"What else did it talk about?" Annie asks, hoping against hope.

"In terms of explosive revelations, you mean?" Katia takes a moment to think. "The rest was almost unchanged from first draft. Less complimentary in tone, perhaps, but positive overall."

The conversation winds down after that. Rose thanks Katia for being so forthcoming and hangs up.

"That was, shall we say, entertaining." Annie stares at Rose, not daring to voice her main takeaway.

Rose stares back. "It was, wasn't it?"

Annie's phone rings. It's Gabriel, delivering on his promise to look at Elinor's autopsy report. The ME was definite in his conclusions. Elinor's toxicology had been clean. There were no suspicious marks on her body and no defensive wounds. She had no scrapes, bruises, or cuts aside from a few small ones caused by the glass from the broken jar. Her death was undoubtedly caused by inhaling too much ground cinnamon.

Annie thanks him and hangs up with a growing sense of desperation.

Rose grabs her own phone. "We have another lead to follow up on!"

"What lead?"

"We know that Lionel suspects Dany had shared another secret with Elinor, but Elinor wasn't ready to talk about it..." Rose strokes her chin, thinking.

Annie nods. "You think Dany's other secret could be related to René's death?"

"It's possible."

"Whatever it was, Elinor didn't include it in her article, so we'll never know."

Rose wags her forefinger. "Not so fast! What if she wrote it up as a separate piece and saved it on the cloud?"

"You think we could break into her cloud?"

"No chance. We don't have those kinds of skills."

Annie draws her eyebrows together. "Then what?"

Rose searches for something on her phone. "I had a feeling we might want to talk to Elinor's parents at some point, so I asked Lionel for their number."

"Did he give it to you?"

"Matter of fact, he did." Rose presses the Call button.

After a few rings, a man picks up.

Rose introduces herself, explains the connection, then asks, "Monsieur Hugonet, were you in the room when your father revealed some secrets to Elinor shortly before his death?"

"No."

"Do you know what those secrets were?"

"His politics, I assume," he says. "I was never interested in that stuff."

*Shame,* Annie thinks to herself.

Rose tries again, "Have you requested access to Elinor's digital assets yet?"

"We haven't," he replies. "And I don't intend to."

"But her files might—"

"Don't call this number again," he cuts her off, his voice a hot whisper. "My wife has barely left the house in six months. She's in bed most of the day, looking at family albums and Elie's childhood diaries. I fear I might lose her to grief."

He hangs up.

"Oh, God." Rose sets her phone down, her eyes glistening.

After a few minutes of heavy silence, Annie feels she's ready to voice what's on her mind. "Our investigation is stuck."

"*Stuck* is such a strong, negative word," Rose begins. "I'd call this a setback, or a plateau, or—" Interrupting herself, she waves a hand in defeat. "Yeah, we're stuck."

# CHAPTER 29

*A*nnie had been hoping that Rose would protest and assure her they weren't stuck and then pull a rabbit, aka a hot new lead, out of her hat. Instead, Rose agreed with her. And now Annie feels completely demoralized.

*Was it all in vain?*

Over the last month, the pair of them traveled around France, went to Monaco, and talked to all manner of people, from billionaires to former gangsters. They learned a lot from those conversations, and from the research conducted with their grandchildren's help. They uncovered hidden truths about the Chantomes, the Gimberts, the Poupons and the Hugonets. But ultimately, they didn't get any closer to solving René's murder than they'd been a month ago.

"Do you think we're fighting a lost cause?" Annie asks Rose. "Do you think René's case is too cold, and we never stood a chance?"

*Am I going to die with that heartache?*

Rose begins to say something, when Lady springs up from her slumber and zooms out of the room. It sounds like someone is opening the door. Annie shoots Rose a concerned look, but Rose doesn't seem worried. Annie strains her ears. Lady's barking isn't threatening. She doesn't growl. She yaps in delight.

"Give me a hug! Oh, yes! You're such a good girl!" A few minutes later, a disheveled Julie lets herself into the sunroom. She greets Annie and Rose and pulls up a third chair. Rose fetches another teacup.

"I was hoping to catch you here," Julie says to Annie before turning to Rose. "Remember how you asked me to look into the lead investigator on Grégoire Lacaze's murder, Commissaire Richard Frinnier?"

Rose blinks. It looks like she's forgotten all about it—just like Annie.

"Gabriel checked his record. Frinnier's clean," Julie reminds them. "There was no reason to believe he'd be the one who destroyed the witness testimonies claiming René had been obsessed with Bernadette."

Annie and Rose nod.

Julie's eyes sparkle. "Flo, Eric, and I did some more digging into our good commissaire Frinnier to see if anything in his past would point in the direction of the missing pages."

"And?" Rose asks. "Did you find dirt? Was he bent?"

Julie gives her a teasing smile. "No. But he was from Yvoire."

"Is that a bad thing?" Annie asks.

"Of course not!" Julie chuckles. "It's a delightful medieval town of one thousand souls on Lake Geneva."

Annie peers at her, confused.

"You know who else was from Yvoire?" Julie asks. "Dany Hugonet! They were born the same year."

Annie gasps.

Julie goes on, "What are the chances that two boys born

the same year in a town of one thousand people would know each other and hang out together?"

"Pretty high, I'd say," Rose offers.

"That's what we thought, too," Julie says. "And that is why I tasked Flo with digging a little deeper. And you know what she found?"

"What?" Annie and Rose ask in unison.

Julie opens her purse, pulls out a folded sheet of paper and shows it to them. It's a copy of an old article from a regional newspaper.

Annie reads the headline. "Dany Hugonet, 12, Saves Classmate Richard Frinnier from Drowning in Lake Geneva." She looks up from the paper. "If the missing testimony was Dany's, then Frinnier had a reason to destroy it. He would've felt morally obligated to help Dany out, wouldn't he?"

"I think he would," Julie agrees. "False testimony is a crime, especially in a murder case. Dany could've gone to prison for that."

"And so, to protect Dany, Frinnier removed his testimony from the file," Annie says.

"I believe he did more than that," Rose says. "The decision to trust Dany's outlier statement that gave René a motive to kill Grégoire was left to Frinnier's discretion."

Annie gesticulates excitedly. "But of course! We couldn't understand why the police had ignored Marie's and Bernadette's testimonies in this regard. Wouldn't they know the relationship between René and Grégoire better than Dany, who wasn't a close friend of theirs?"

Rose narrows her eyes. "When I spoke with Marie, she referred to 'testimonies'—plural—that contradicted hers. That means at least two, right? Who do you think the second liar was?"

Annie slaps her thighs. "Etienne Poupon!"

The three of them exchange loaded looks as a realization sinks in.

Julie begins cautiously, "Assuming it was them, why would Dany and Etienne give false testimonies incriminating René in Grégoire's murder?"

Silence sets in. No one wants to voice the obvious conclusion.

Squaring her shoulders, Annie takes it upon herself. "Because they were the murderers! They'd killed Grégoire, framed René for it, and then staged René's suicide."

"What was their motive?" Julie asks.

"To save Etienne's reputation and possibly PRAC," Rose says. "René must've found out about Joel Gimbert's money."

"How?" Annie asks.

"I don't know yet," Rose replies. "But if we join forces and use all our brainpower, I'm sure we'll figure it out."

"René likely gave Etienne and Dany an ultimatum," Julie picks up. "Either they returned the tainted money, or René would tell the world how the hottest anti-capitalist party on the block was funded by the country's most predatory capitalist."

"That would be a very René thing to do," Annie says.

Rose turns to her. "We cracked the case, girl! It may be a challenge to prove Dany's and Etienne's guilt, but we unraveled the mystery."

"We did, didn't we?" Annie rubs her breastbone, letting the notion sink in.

"You were damn right to come to me with your case," Rose enthuses. "You have your answers now."

As Annie thanks her and Julie for everything, a weird phenomenon occurs. The atoms that make up the universe begin to rearrange themselves. With tiny jerks, the world around Annie starts to revolve on its axis until it completes a half circle and comes to a stop.

Annie already experienced this once before on January 4, 1961, when her world turned upside down. Today, on the eve of the anniversary of René's death, it flipped again, right side up.

*At last.*

# CHAPTER 30

*D*ressed in her best coat, complete with a new scarf and hat, Annie waits for Rose to call her and tell her she's outside the house. Rose will drive Annie to the Mazargues Cemetery in Marseilles so she can lay flowers on René's grave.

It's been Annie's annual ritual ever since he died. On All Saints' Day, she'd visit her parents' and siblings' graves, and then Andre's after he passed in the Saint-Pierre Cemetery. Typically, one or both of her daughters will accompany her. But on the anniversary of René's death, she'd go to Mazargues, alone. Recently though, as her health declined, it would be one of her grandsons who'd drive her there.

And this year on this quiet morning of January 4, it will be Rose. They'll stop on their way at Annie's old florist friend, get the bouquets, and drive on to Mazargues. And then they'll have tea and cookies at Simone's teahouse, before Rose returns Annie home and heads back to Beldoc.

Annie's phone pings with a text message.

Your chauffeur is parking.

Smiling, Annie decides to head out to Rose. She's too warm with her coat and hat on inside on this side of the door. She crosses the front yard and opens the gate latch. Stepping onto the sidewalk of her residential alley, she looks around. Rose is nowhere in sight. Annie scans the street for Rose's unmistakable yellow car but can't see it.

*Did she park it around the corner?*

Annie's one-way street doesn't have any empty spots. The cars are lined up so tightly their bumpers are French kissing. The metaphor makes Annie smile as she acknowledges the "before and after Rose" in her life. It's undeniable.

Right on cue, Rose appears from around the corner, slightly out of breath.

"Had to park in Timbuktu," she complains, pointing vaguely down the street. "Not a spot to be found."

"That's what I thought."

"But don't worry, lean on me if your knee is acting up."

"Don't worry, dear." Annie lifts her cane. "This old friend will be enough. Just bear with me if I'm slow."

They shuffle down the sleepy street with Rose adjusting her pace to Annie's—something she didn't do when they walked on the beach in Le Crotoy.

*Could there be a "before and after Annie" in Rose's life, too, or am I being presumptuous?*

Suddenly, a male figure in a mask and gloves lunges from behind a tree, making a grab for Rose. "You're coming with me!"

Rose pushes him back and plunges a hand into her purse.

"Don't even think about it!" The man grips the purse, barking at Annie, "If you try to scream or call the cops, you're dead!"

Rose holds on to her purse for dear life—as does the much stronger attacker. He begins to retreat, pulling her away with him like a wolf dragging a pugnacious sheep. Time seems to slow for Annie. Her heart is racing, but her mind is clearer than ever. She tightens her grip on her cane, Gabriel's voice ringing in her head, *You got this, Medz Mama! Just like we practiced, remember?*

With a strength that surprises her, Annie swings her cane. It whistles through the air and makes a resounding thwack as it connects with the assailant's shins. His legs buckle. He lets out a yelp and staggers, grimacing in pain and swearing that he's going to kill Annie.

Rose groans and yanks her purse from the man's weakened clutch.

Acting fast, like Gabriel taught her, Annie inverts the cane and pivots her body. Still reeling from the first blow, the man barely has time to react as Annie raises her cane higher.

*Use your weight to add force to your arms.*

With a grunt, Annie brings the solid handle of the cane crashing down into the assailant's groin. His eyes bulge, and a strangled scream escapes his lips.

Annie glances at Rose who's screaming "Help!" and rummaging in her purse, probably for her phone to call the police. Still fueled by adrenaline, Annie takes a step back to gauge her next move. The man is doubled over, clutching his groin, howling, and cursing. He casts a furious, bloodshot gaze at Annie and unsheathes a knife.

Annie attacks at once. With a battle cry to make a warrior proud, she thrusts the cane forward, like a spear, targeting the man's solar plexus. As the heavy handle sinks into his chest, the air whooshes out of him and he crumples to the ground.

"Step back!" Rose shouts at Annie.

Pulling her away from the man, Rose whips an uncommonly thick red-and-white candy cane out of her purse. She extends her arm, turns away and sprays the man's face with a pungent cloud from the straight end of her candy cane.

*I'll be damned, it's pepper spray!*

The man bawls in agony, rubbing at his eyes with the balls of his palms.

Rose drags Annie farther away from the man, all while shouting out for help. The street begins to stir. Three or four figures appear in the distance and rush toward them. One turns out to be Annie's neighbor. The others look like tourists. After checking that Annie and Rose are all right, the new arrivals try to restrain the attacker. Coughing from the acrid smoke, they give up when he points his knife at them. Annie's neighbor calls the police.

The man scrambles to his feet and runs to one of the cars parked by the sidewalk. Caned and sprayed, he's a bit slow to start his car. Rose uses the opportunity to snap a picture of the license plate number before he finally drives off.

Annie pulls her phone out. "I'm calling Gabriel!"

"I'm sending him the plate number," Rose says. "You're a badass, by the way!"

As they wait for the gendarmes and Gabriel, Annie feels her adrenaline dropping. Propped by Rose from one side and her neighbor from the other, she's pretty shaken. But she's also elated. A sense of pride and profound satisfaction comes over her.

*I stood up to the bad guy and held my ground!*

Her cane, the symbol of her fragility, became a sword that she wielded like a seasoned knight protecting a damsel in distress. The damsel in question—Rose—took an active part in her own rescue. Not only did she ward off the attacker's attempt to abduct her, but she gave him a candy cane treatment he won't forget.

We're living proof, Annie thinks to herself, that vigilantism can be practiced at any age, provided one is sufficiently reckless and desperate.

# CHAPTER 31

*I*nstinctively, Rose adjusts her pace to the rhythm of the tambourines, as the Epiphany procession snakes through the old town's cobblestone streets. Like other processions throughout Provence, Beldoc's March of the Magi Kings pays homage to the Three Wise Men who traveled to Bethlehem from countries far, far away to worship baby Jesus.

For this occasion, Rose donned her Arlésienne costume, with a padded down vest over it, and gave Lady a sequined body warmer. Treading beside Rose, Sarah is dressed up, too. Her unsuccessful attempts to keep Baxter from sticking his nose into Lady's derrière make Flo giggle.

Taking pity on Sarah, Rose picks up Lady to give Baxter time to sublimate his ardor into a demurer pursuit.

Baxter's BFF Harley jogs proudly next to Karl. He displays much more dignity than the purebred pug, despite the gold paper tinsels dangling from his collar.

But it's Karl himself who's the undisputed star of Rose's group. Draped in an improvised cape and carrying a scepter made from a broomstick, he's the Wise Man of the Streets. The title was bestowed upon him by the mayor himself some twenty minutes ago, when the march set out from the central post office. Victor and his staffers are at the head now, leading the crowd.

What with being a lifelong atheist and diehard secularist, this is the first time that Victor is doing the Epiphany procession. In the little speech he gave before the kickoff, he went to great lengths to explain how his involvement is only about building the community and the cultural side of things.

Rose doesn't quite buy it. She suspects that Victor's sister Marlene has a finger in this pie. A former nun who still lives and works at a monastery, she'd been estranged from her brother for the longest time. But two years ago at Christmas, Marlene and her son reconnected with Victor following an incident that could've cost the youth his life.

This Epiphany procession is a first for Rose, too.

While she loves the tasting of the *brioche des rois*, Rose had never joined Sarah, who does the Epiphany march every year. "I believe in Karma," Rose would tell her. "Can we do a Buddhist procession?" But this year, she showed up, albeit still a little shaken from the attack two days ago. Indeed, what better way to neutralize any residual ripple from that shock wave than by partaking in a holy march for cake?

*Or maybe it's Annie's influence?*

The old girl couldn't come to Beldoc today. She's celebrating the Armenian Orthodox Christmas with her family in Cassis.

Julie is not marching with Rose or spending time with Gabriel and Annie in Cassis this year. She's too busy at the shop, looking to close her best holiday season ever.

*That's my girl!*

Flo turns to Rose. "I still can't believe it wasn't Blaise Gimbert who'd sent that guy to intimidate you! I was so sure it was him!"

"Me too," Sarah chimes in. "When I learned that the

gendarmes had found the car and arrested your attacker, I was certain he was Gimbert's man."

"I was surprised they were able to find him," Flo says. "I'd expected the license plate to be fake and the car stolen."

Rose relays Gabriel's explanation. "The way most dealers do it these days is as effective but much less risky. They travel to Eastern Europe and take out a long-term lease with a foreign company that retains ownership of the car. This allows them to never pay fines or speeding tickets, which are sent to the company, which doesn't pay them and doesn't share the driver's name."

"Then how did the police nab the guy?"

"By leveraging insurance regulations," Rose says. "They found the car and towed it to the impound lot. The foreign company had to reveal the renter's name to be able to collect it."

Sarah grins. "How clever of them!"

"I also feared the guy wouldn't talk," Flo says.

Rose puts her chin up. "But he did, and he led the gendarmes to the person that no one expected or suspected."

"That person was the brother of the blondie you met at the PRAC fundraiser, right?" Sarah asks.

"Her name is Louise Tapiero," Rose offers. "The guy who attacked us was a former colleague of her brother's. Sammy Tapiero had paid him to do the dirty job."

"I've always wondered," Flo says, rubbing her nose, "how people go about delegating the dirty jobs. Do they post ads?"

Rose chuckles. "Sammy didn't need to. Before he followed his sister into politics, he'd been a small-time drug dealer. The man who attacked me still is."

"Do you think he would've killed you?" Sarah asks, her expression terrorized.

"He swears he was just going to slap me hard enough to scare me into letting go of this case."

Sarah snorts. "And we're supposed to believe him!"

"How did Louise know you were looking into Elinor's death?" Flo asks.

"After Annie and I spoke with Katia, she told Mikel about our call, and about the questions we'd asked in relation to Elinor's death," Rose explains.

Flo narrows her eyes. "But then Mikel could've been in on the attack, too."

"I don't think so," Rose says.

"Because he's drop-dead gorgeous, so he can't be a bad person?" Flo teases Rose.

With a glance at Baxter, Rose sets Lady down. "No, because both Katia and Lionel believe he's a good person, and I happen to like and trust both of them."

Flo and Sarah exchange a skeptical look.

"Mikel's being so easy on the eye doesn't hurt, I suppose," Rose admits. "But consider this. Katia has never told him how she feels about Louise, because she doesn't want to come across as insecure and jealous."

"How is that relevant?" Flo asks.

"If Mikel knew about Katia's suspicions, he probably wouldn't have relayed my conversation with Katia to Louise," Rose says.

"Why did he do that?"

"She's become one of his most trusted advisors over the past few months," Rose replies. "And, like I said, he had no idea how much his wife distrusts and resents her."

Flo nods. "So, Louise Tapiero learns from Mikel that you're looking into the circumstances of Elinor's death. For some unclear reason, she panics and shares her fears with her unsavory brother Sammy."

"Right."

"Why did she panic?" Flo shoots Rose a narrow look. "She and her brother are relative newcomers to PRAC, completely unrelated to Dany Hugonet or Etienne Poupon."

"She told the police she worried for Mikel's image and PRAC's future," Rose says. "What she did was a preemptive action to protect both."

Flo sneers. "Such devotion to the leader! Such initiative and self-sacrifice for the cause!"

"It does seem a bit over the top, doesn't it?" Rose concurs while keeping an eye on Baxter, who seems to have given up on courting Lady for now.

Flo lifts her eyes skyward. "More than a bit."

"Let's get back to our chronology," Sarah says. "So, Louise shares her concerns with her brother Sammy, who reassures her he'll scare the grannies into abandoning their investigation."

Flo nudges her playfully. "But the grannies had a few tricks up their sleeves, huh?"

The procession turns onto rue de l'Andouillette and the business district. As they pass Julie's shop, Rose spots her and Eric behind the counter, waving at them through the window. She waves back. Flo gives them a thumbs-up.

Movement across the street draws Rose's attention to Igor's bookshop. He's outside with a guitar. Magda, the owner of the adjacent Lavender Dream boutique, is standing next to him, hugging a guitar of her own.

The procession slows down and halts.

"We're going to perform everybody's favorite scout song about three boys," Igor announces. "It felt like a fitting choice to celebrate the three Magi."

"Everybody's welcome to sing along," Magda adds.

Rose points at her guitar. "I had no idea you played!"

"I didn't." She glances at Igor. "He's been teaching me."

Igor strums a few chords, and then Magda joins in. They begin to sing "Ils étaient trois garçons." Rose, Karl, Flo, Mayor

Jacquet, his secretary Chantal, newsdealer Adonis, and many others in the procession start to hum along. The chilly air feels warmer as Igor leads with his deep voice. Magda's tones, husky from decades of smoking, add a surprisingly pleasant harmony.

Soon enough, there's an entire chorus of voices accompanying the leads. Some are humming, while others are belting out lyrics at top volume. Many clap their hands, others snap their fingers in rhythm with the beat. Everyone is swaying together. Even those like Sarah, who don't know the lyrics by heart, are stomping out beats with their feet.

As Igor and Magda finish playing the last chord, the procession members give them a hearty round of applause before continuing on their way.

Five minutes later, they reach the *Place de la mairie*, where two makeshift tables are set next to each other in front. On one of them are three oversized, colorful *brioches des rois* cakes and three shiny paper crowns. The second table displays a large selection of Nativity manger figurines.

Victor and Rose advance to stand on either side of the tables.

"Ladies first," Victor says in an unexpected show of gallantry.

Rose begins, pointing at the figurines, "The santons on display were all made by the *santonniers* of Beldoc and the surrounding villages. Will our talented craftspeople please step forward so we can acknowledge them?"

Three men and a woman come out of the crowd and bow. Everyone cheers.

"Will you say a word or two about the santons for the sake of the children in our procession?" Rose asks them.

The men nudge the woman forward.

"The word *santon* comes from *little saint* in Provençal," she says. "The tradition was born after the French

Revolution, when the religion and life-size Nativity scenes were banned."

One of her fellow craftsmen surveys the crowd. "Do prohibitions ever work in Provence?"

"Neeever!!!" everyone shouts.

With a grin, the woman continues, "So, instead of live performances, the people shrank the Nativity characters into tiny figurines, and Christmas mangers went underground. Eventually, the ban was lifted, but the santons became part of the Provençal way of life."

She bows to show that she finished her talk.

After the applause dies down, Victor takes the floor, "This year's brioches were sponsored by Aline's, Julie's, and Heinrich's bakeries."

"All three contain gluten though," Rose butts in. "If you want a gluten-free version to take home, you know where to find my granddaughter's shop!"

"Please form a line while I slice up the cakes," Victor adds. "The three lucky individuals that get the slice with a broad bean hidden inside will be crowned king or queen for the rest of the day."

Chantal counts the heads and turns to Victor. "One hundred three."

"If you get the bean," Victor warns as he cuts the buttery cake into narrow slices, "don't say anything until everyone has had a slice."

The yummy-looking brioche, with its golden-brown crust and fluffy center, makes Rose's mouth water. But Victor, Chantal, and Rose have decided to forgo their shares to make sure they don't win. They pass out slices until everybody has one in their hands. The crowd is buzzing with excitement as they bite into their pieces.

"I have the bean!" three distinct voices cry out.

Rose seeks out the winners in the crowd. One of them is Karl!

Victor gestures for them to come forward and show him their beans. When he verifies the winners, he snatches up the paper crowns from the table and places them atop each winner's head, proclaiming them king or queen.

Rose smiles to herself. *How unrepublican of you,* Monsieur le Maire!

The crowd erupts into cheers.

"*Longo maï!*" someone shouts in Provençal.

Others join in. "*Vive le roi! Vive la reine!*"

"Long live the Wise King of the Streets!" Flo yells.

"As part of this year's royal package," Victor says to the winners, "you get a santon, too. Pick one among those on display."

Karl stares at him. "For free?"

"Courtesy of our santon makers," Victor says, pointing toward them.

They bow.

"Everybody else is invited to purchase one after the winners have had their pick," Rose informs the public.

Victor points at Karl. "You go first."

As if in a trance, Karl moves to the table that houses dozens of handmade and hand-painted clay figurines. Only Provence could come up with such a wild mix of the banal and the biblical, Rose thinks to herself. Fishermen, shepherds, bakers and millers mingle with angels, Mary, Joseph, and baby Jesus. The all-time favorites such as the Three Wise Men, the blind couple, the pétanque player, and the huntsman have made room for new characters representing contemporary occupations and pastimes.

Karl combs through the collection in search of something.

"Found it!" he exclaims as he grabs a figurine and holds it up. "This is my favorite santon."

Rose peers. It's a male character with his arms thrown up. Must be the *ravi*. The ravi is the village idiot to most people. Some believe he's a mystic.

Once the other two royals have picked their santons, the remaining ones sell out fairly quickly. The procession resumes. Ten minutes later, it reaches the church, its final stop. Some of the marchers go straight in. Others, including Rose, Flo and Karl linger outside, chatting.

Unobtrusively, Rose watches Karl. He looks happy in his paper crown and bedsheet cape, with the broomstick staff in one hand and the *ravi* santon in the other. She's itching to ask him, *Which ravi are you, the simpleton or the mystic?*

But as she opens her mouth, she realizes it's a dumb question. Because, in Karl's case, they are the same.

# CHAPTER 32

*R*ose steps into Sarah's cozy living room, where the scent of Earl Grey and vanilla cupcakes envelops her. Lady dashes in behind her, tail wagging. Sarah's pug, Baxter, waddles over to greet them.

"Ah, Rose! You made it!" Sarah exclaims.

"Namaste!" Rose joins her palms and bows to all five book club ladies. "Wouldn't miss it for the world!"

She takes a seat next to Colette, a petite woman with a penchant for colorful scarves with birds on them. Her today's choice is psychedelic peacock.

Across from Rose sits Anne-Sophie, a librarian with an encyclopedic knowledge of literature.

"We'll pick up right where we left off before Christmas," she says, pushing her round glasses up on her nose. "Let's talk about Countess Ellen Olenska's character in the *Age of Innocence.*"

Sarah pours tea into delicate china cups. "I love her. The way she sacrificed her own happiness is so noble and so tragic!"

Marie-Jo strokes the book on her lap. "I agree with the

noble and tragic. She gave up her chance at happiness to save Newland's reputation and marriage. But I wonder if it was necessary..."

Colette sets her hand against her heart. "Ah, the beautiful things we women do for love!"

"When you say, 'beautiful things,' do you mean *crazy shit*?" shopkeeper Magda asks her.

Colette shrugs. "Potato, potahto."

"What do you think, Rose?" Sarah hands Rose a cup of tea. "Was Ellen's sacrifice necessary?"

Rose takes her glasses off. "Leaving the personal aspect aside, the societal pressures on women in the 1870s New York didn't leave Ellen much choice, did they?"

"Well, she had the option of being like Sarah of *The French Lieutenant's Woman*," Anne-Sophie says with a wink. "In 1870s, she and Newland would be ostracized, but she wouldn't be burned at the stake. Those days were over."

Sarah clenches her fists. "Not everywhere. In some places, women get hanged or stoned for less."

Putting things into a broader perspective is Sarah's specialty, and Rose loves that about her.

The women nod, their faces darkening.

Baxter gets up and launches yet another attempt at pursuing Lady. Sarah scoops him up.

"Back to Ellen," Collette says, "it doesn't help that Newland chooses societal norms over true love early in the story, but also at the end."

Magda looks up from her copy of the book. "In his defense, he isn't in love yet at the beginning, and at the end, he finds out that his wife is pregnant with his child."

"I agree; he did some sacrificing, too." Rose sets her glasses down on the coffee table. "What if Ellen was the opposite of noble? What if she was cunning and manipulative, like... a femme fatale?"

*I was going to say, "like Louise."*

The room falls into thoughtful silence. Rose tries to refocus on Edith Wharton's book, but she can't anymore. Her thoughts have drifted to Annie's case, and there is no bringing them back.

*How far would Louise go to protect Mikel's image?*

Anne-Sophie raises an eyebrow. "Well, that would be a different story altogether!"

The book club delves back into the discussion, but Rose's mind is elsewhere.

At the PRAC fete, Louise flattered Mikel shamelessly. She was actively seducing a married man. A married who has a child to boot! Her behavior was shabby, even from a contemporary perspective. And when compared to Ellen Olenska's, who decided to return to Poland when she learned about May's pregnancy, it was downright dishonorable.

Would a woman like Louise, a woman intent on ruining her love interest's happy marriage, do "crazy shit" just to protect his reputation? Would someone so shallow put herself in danger for another person, even for a man she thinks she loves?

It isn't that Louise sent a thug to intimidate Rose that seems off. It's that she took such a risk for Mikel. And not to save his life, but simply to shield him from negative fallout, should the news of PRAC's ultra-capitalist sponsor come out.

The more plausible course of action for Louise would've been to try to prevail upon Elinor to withdraw her article. That's what Rose had suspected Katia of trying to do, before she learned Katia sought the exact opposite, hoping to save her marriage. That's why she'd gone to Elinor's—to persuade her to publish her exposé.

*Why hadn't Louise tried to talk sense into Elinor?*

Well, maybe she had. Maybe she'd done it at the PRAC office, on the sidelines of a rally, or during a fete. Perhaps over the phone. Or in person, by going to Elinor's, like Katia had done.

Rose realizes that the discussion is over when a chorus of thank-yous and goodbyes forces her to tune in. She thanks Sarah and heads across the street to her house with Lady in tow.

The moment she's inside, she takes out her phone and dials Gabriel. "Hi, are you at the office?"

"Yes, why?"

"Louise Tapiero, the woman whose brother's pal attacked me, do you know what she looks like?"

"She and her brother Sammy were questioned in Paris, not here," Gabriel says. "But I have the transcript, and I've seen their pictures, since I now have a personal interest in this case."

Rose sits down. "Good. Do you also have access to the CCTV feed from Elinor's street around her time of death?"

"I don't, and depending on the Parisian regulations, that footage may have been deleted by now. But I can ask Commissaire Zaoui."

"Zaoui... Oh, right! The officer who'd been looking into Elinor's death before the ME ruled it an accidental."

"Let me call him, and call you back," Gabriel says.

For the next forty-five minutes, Rose performs household chores with the kind of manic energy Lady had when she was a puppy. She starts the washing machine, vacuums, fills the dishwasher, folds bedsheets, and dusts all the surfaces in the living room, all while fighting the temptation to call Annie.

*What if the footage was destroyed? What if it doesn't show what I hoped it would?*

After all, the chance that Louise went to see Elinor that day, shortly after Katia had left, is minimal. It was just a wild guess inspired by the discussion at her book club. It's going to come to nothing, and Rose will have wasted Gabriel's and Zaoui's time.

Rose is regretting her initiative when Gabriel calls her back.

"The footage from that day was deleted after thirty days," he begins. "But Zaoui, that consummate nitpicker, had made a copy for the file. Just in case."

Rose's heart thumps against her ribcage. "And?"

"He connected me to his computer, and we reviewed the segment between Katia Poupon's departure and Elinor Hugonet's death."

"And?"

"According to the ME's report, Elinor died at twelve-thirty p.m." He pauses. "Guess who rushes away from the building at twelve forty-five?"

Rose growls. "You're killing me!"

"Louise Tapiero," he says. "She's on tape leaving Elinor's building with a laptop under her arm fifteen minutes after Elenore's death."

*Oh my God.* "Now the attack on me makes so much more sense! Louise was trying to protect *herself*, not Mikel."

"It's possible."

Rose takes a breath before asking, "Do you think she killed Elinor?"

"Doubtful, in light of the ME's report," Gabriel says. "But Zaoui will reopen the case, and the investigation will tell us what happened. I hope he can prove Louise was in Elinor's apartment at the time of death, and not simply in the building."

"Do you think he can do that?"

"I'm pretty sure he can. The forensic experts will check the clothes Elinor wore that day, the pieces of the jar, all the hairs and threads collected from the death scene for Louise's fingerprints and DNA."

"Wasn't everything already checked the first time around?" Rose asks.

"Not very thoroughly, since the cause of death was established early on, and the case was closed. Besides, no one was looking for a match with Louise Tapiero. She simply wasn't on the radar at the time."

"And now she is."

"Thanks to you," Gabriel says with a smile in his voice. "You're almost as good at this as Julie, you know?"

"Almost? Who do you think gave her the sleuthing genes?"

He laughs at that.

"What if Louise gets lucky?" Rose asks. "What if there is no trace of her presence in the apartment when Elinor died?"

"Louise Tapiero is no hitman trained in cleaning crime scenes," Gabriel says. "If she was with Elinor Hugonet when Elinor died, then she left a trace. And we will find it."

# CHAPTER 33

*I*t's unusually warm for late January. The sun beams down from the clear winter sky, painting René's tomb a golden hue. Annie holds on to her cane and shifts her weight from one leg to the other. A sharp pang shoots up from her bad knee, but she ignores it. Her good knee, which is "good" in comparison only, needs a break.

While Annie comes to René's grave every year, his family, except for Monique, haven't been to the Mazargues Cemetery —or to Marseilles for that matter—in decades.

Nestled in the heart of the bustling, chaotic city, Mazargues is a haven of tranquility. Annie looks around at the immaculately trimmed lawns dotted with glistening white headstones, floral arrangements and potted plants. The air is still, laced with a faint smell of freshly cut grass that serves as a base note to the scent coming off the gorgeous bouquet she's holding.

Annie shifts her gaze to the brass plaque bearing René's name and years of birth and death. Compared to her own long life, his was as brief as a firefly's spark. But he left a trace. He cared deeply. He was loved.

It's been only a week since Rose's eureka about the CCTV footage. But so much happened in that short span of time!

The stars, which had been shifting since the day Annie received Olivia's letter, aligned fully. Commissaire Zaoui reopened Elinor Hugonet's case. Now that the police knew what to look for, they found Louise Tapiero's fingerprints on the pieces of the jar and all over Elinor's home office. Her DNA was found in those same rooms, as well as in the cinnamon collected from the scene.

She was brought in for questioning. Confronted with all the evidence, she broke down and delivered a full confession.

Louise had gone to Elinor's that day. When she arrived, Elinor was busy preparing a cinnamon bun recipe for her food column. She let Louise in and asked her not to disturb her until the buns were in the oven and the timer was on. After that, they could talk.

But Louise was too eager to wait. She told Elinor straight away what a terrible decision it would be to reveal to the world that Blaise Gimbert was funding the revived PRAC...

"What are you going to achieve, huh?" Louise slammed her palm onto the high granite worktop. "Undermine Mikel? Clip his wings, making sure he can't fly as high as he deserves? Ruin his political career?"

"The public deserves to know the truth, so they can make informed decisions about supporting PRAC," Elinor said.

"The public needs PRAC to succeed, not sink!" Louise countered.

"Mikel told me to do what I thought was right," Elinor assured Louise while reaching for a jar. "And Katia insisted I go ahead and publish my article."

*Argh, that sneaky, manipulative bitch!*

In a fit of rage, Louise snatched the jar from Elinor's hand and smashed it against the granite countertop. The impact caused a cloud of cinnamon to fill the air, which Elinor inadvertently inhaled. This led to severe choking and coughing. Louise watched Elinor's face turn a startling shade of red as she gasped for air. Then Elinor's knees buckled under her, and her body hit the floor with a sickening thud.

Louise stumbled back.

Elinor struggled a little longer, clawing at her throat, her face turning blue. Louise didn't move, didn't try to help Elinor, didn't call an ambulance. Moments passed that seemed like an eternity. The gasping stopped. Elinor lay still on the floor, her eyes wide open and glassy, her chest still.

As if watching herself in a movie, Louise ran to Elinor's home office. She searched all the drawers and cabinets. None were locked, as luck would have it. She didn't find any printouts of the article. Desperate, she grabbed Elinor's laptop and ran out the door.

According to Gabriel, Louise's actions don't qualify as murder or manslaughter. But, while Elinor's death from breathing in too much cinnamon dust was accidental, Louise is still criminally liable because she failed to provide assistance to Elinor. According to the French Penal Code, when assistance can be provided without taking disproportionate risks, failing to do so is an offense. Louise would have in no way endangered herself by trying to help Elinor. Yet, she chose not to move a finger where it was her duty to help.

The fact that she then searched Elinor's office and stole her laptop, not to mention instigating the attack on Rose later, guarantees that she will be charged with several crimes. She's looking at a few years in prison.

After Louise was arrested, Rose received two back-to-back phone calls. The first one was from Katia who thanked her and Annie for unmasking Louise and saving her marriage.

The second one was from Elinor's parents. Lionel had

told them about Louise. They called Rose to let her know how grateful they were for the truth about Elinor's last moments. It gave them comfort that the person who had caused the accident—and who let Elinor die—was found and will be brought to justice.

Before hanging up, they asked for Rose's postal address to send her something through the mail. It turned out to be a copy of Dany's memoir, the one he'd given to Elinor on his deathbed. Too shocked by the confessions it contained, Elinor had decided she needed some time to come to terms with who her beloved grandpa really was. And so, she locked the memoir in her parents' safe box and asked them not to read it yet.

A birdsong somewhere above René's grave pulls Annie back into the present moment. She looks around. Her heart overflows with gratitude as her eyes fall on Rose who's standing beside her.

*You did it, my friend! You cracked René's case.*

Without Rose's energy, doggedness and creativity, Annie would've never been able to investigate a dozen suspects living all over the country—or six feet under for some. She would've never figured out who killed René, let alone found new evidence to prove it. And now, Rose and Annie are going to tell Monique and Jacques the truth about what happened to René in January 1961.

Annie's gaze travels to the Chantomes, all of whom are here. The women—Monique, Hélène, and Olivia—couldn't prevail upon Jacques to come down to Marseilles with them. In the end, it was Armand who found the right words to get his recalcitrant grandpa to be part of this journey.

As inconspicuously as she can, Annie glances over at Jacques. He stands apart from the group, his expression stern. His eyes fixed on the headstone are the exact same shade of blue as René's.

*How come I never realized it until now?*

Monique is rooted in place next to Annie. She's gazing at the headstone, a beautiful bouquet in her arms. The younger generations of the family, represented by Hélène, Olivia, and Armand, stand close together in respectful silence one step behind Monique.

Monique's eyes glisten as she lifts them to Rose. There is no need for words.

Monique and Annie step forward and lay their flowers on René's grave. As they straighten up, Annie can feel Jacques' eyes on her. Last night on the phone, she promised him a series of revelations that would turn his world upside down. He responded with a disparaging snort and a quip that he didn't care for another baseless theory of hers.

But now he's watching her, anxious. Intrigued. He's been thinking about this, perhaps even doubting.

He's ready for the truth.

# CHAPTER 34

*A* short time later, they walk away from René's grave and clamber into cars, Annie riding with Rose. They drive off to Simone's Teahouse, an unpretentious teahouse not far from the cemetery.

The founding owner of that place, Simone, was a good friend of Annie's when Annie lived in Marseilles. Simone passed away about a decade ago. Her lovely granddaughter Camille, who now runs the place, leads Annie's group to the back room where a table was booked for brunch. This isn't a private room, but it's spacious enough to have some privacy without relinquishing the welcome background noise supplied by the chatter of other patrons.

As they sit down, Jacques and Monique pick seats as far apart from each other as possible, just like they'd done during the dinner at Les Tonneaux. Rose nudges Annie toward the head of the table, taking a seat next to her.

The hot drinks arrive first. Annie adds milk and honey to her tea, hoping it will keep the rust out of her voice. She and Rose have much to say to the Chantomes.

Jacques gives her a defiant look. "If you're going to rock my world, I suggest you get started."

She looks at him, then at the rest of his family. "The police have officially cleared René of Grégoire Lacaze's murder. The records are being updated, and you'll be hearing from them soon."

A stunned silence settles over the table.

It reigns supreme until Monique exhales a loud *Ha!* and turns to Jacques. "I knew it! I always knew it in my heart!"

Everybody's eyes are on Annie. While Jacques has gone into a torpor, the others bombard her with questions. They want to know how, when, why, and who the real killer was. They want to know everything.

"René didn't kill himself either," Annie says. "The two monsters who had strangled Grégoire came back a few days later, killed René, and made it look like a suicide."

More questions ensue.

Annie lifts her hand, palm forward. "Before we get to that, I want to clarify another point, the one concerning René's 'shady dealings' with the Mob."

"Let me guess," Monique jumps in, "the Mob had nothing to do with any of it, right?"

"They did, but not the way Jacques had deduced." Annie shifts her eyes to Jacques.

He holds her gaze. "Tell me."

"In 1959, a then powerful crime syndicate known as the French Connection, approached your father with an offer to launder a large sum of money from a heroin sale. Auction houses are perfect for that, you see," Annie begins.

Jacques shakes his head. "Papa would've never agreed to become a banker for Le Milieu."

"That position is called *saraf* in Le Milieu," Rose interjects. "Annie and I interviewed Napoleon Albertini, aka

ANA T. DREW

Big Napo, the only participant in René's kidnapping still alive."

Annie picks up, "They assured Pierre-François that it would be a one-off. He was in a tight spot at the time, due to several costly mistakes by his assessors. So, he said yes to the one-off."

"How could he be so naive?" Monique wonders, lifting her eyes skyward.

Annie nods. "That misguided move set in motion a series of events that culminated in the kidnapping of René in order to force Pierre-François' hand and make him work for the Mob on a regular basis."

"Paul and Mémé Leoni gave Pierre-François seventy-two hours and threatened to kill René if the police got involved," Rose adds.

Jacques begins to say something but his voice cracks.

He stops, takes a breath and tries again. "I don't understand. If Papa agreed to the offer, which he must have, since we got René back, then why did we subsequently go bankrupt?"

"You didn't," Annie says with a soft smile. "Your father had learned from his earlier mistake. This time around he took a better course of action and avoided enslaving himself and his family to the Mafia."

"What did he do?" several Chantomes ask at once.

"He used the three days he was given to liquidate all his assets, including the auction house, and offer all the proceeds, in cash, to Le Milieu in exchange for René," Annie replies.

Jacques leans back in his chair. "Smart move! No Mafia boss can resist an offer like that. Even one that already has more cash on his hands than he can launder."

"Besides, with the auction house gone, your father wasn't valuable to them anymore," Annie says. "So, they took the money and released René."

A long silence follows during which the Chantomes process what they just heard while Annie and Rose sip their tea.

Monique turns to Jacques. "All this time, you'd assumed the worst about René. Why? You knew him as well as I did. What made you think he'd get mixed up with the Mob?"

"We also knew Papa, didn't we?" Jacques parries before letting out a shaggy sigh. "I'd just pieced things together, you know? Our parents' turmoil, the hushed phone calls, then René turned up in a sorry state, Maman and Papa fussing over him, and everybody keeping mum about what had happened."

"I get it," Monique says. "You connected the dots, and you weren't that far off. What I don't get is why you'd choose to suspect René, rather than Papa, of shady dealings that got him in trouble?"

"What did you think that trouble was, by the way?" Hélène asks her dad.

"I had all sorts of theories," Jacques replies, "from card debts to causing a deadly accident by carrying out some political stunt for PRAC."

Olivia chimes in, "Personally, I would've assumed that René had been kidnapped for ransom by criminals who knew his father was rich."

"That sort of thing didn't happen back then," Jacques explains to his granddaughter. "Unless you ran with the Mob, Marseilles was a damn safe place back in 1960."

Armand flashes him a dreamy smile. "Good times!"

"Besides," Jacques continues, "I thought, if René had done nothing wrong, then why all the secrecy after he was returned to us? There is no shame in paying a ransom for a kidnapped child, so why not tell us?"

Annie sets her cup down. "Now you know why. Your family's financial ruin was the price your father paid for his own sins, not for René's."

Jacques nods slowly before turning to Monique. "I didn't really answer your question about why I blamed René rather than Papa." His jaw trembles. "It was envy. René was better than me in every way. I knew that. And I resented him for it."

"You shouldn't have," Monique says, before turning to Annie. "He was better than ninety-nine percent of humanity, wouldn't you agree?"

Annie shakes her head. "I'd say ninety-nine-point-ninety-nine percent."

With a smile, Monique turns back to Jacques. "Try to swap your envy for pride. I've always felt that way about him. And Annie, too, I'm sure."

"Dear Annie," Hélène presses both her hands to her chest. "I have never seen my dad and my aunt talk to each other without an intermediary. How can I ever thank you for that?"

Annie grins. "You don't need to thank me. It makes me happy to see this."

"What about the murder and the suicide?" Armand reminds her. "Can you tell us more?"

Olivia leans forward. "I can't wait to discover the truth!"

"That truth would've never seen the light of day without my friend Rose, so I will let her explain the how," Annie says.

All heads turn toward Rose.

She pulls a plastic-bound document from her tote bag. "This is a copy of Dany Hugonet's handwritten memoir."

"Who is Dany Hugonet?" Armand asks.

"The man who cofounded the Party of Radical Anti-Capitalists together with Etienne Poupon," Rose replies.

Hélène shoots a glance at Monique. "Uncle René was an active member, wasn't he?"

"To our parents' chagrin," Monique confirms.

"Shortly before he died, Dany gave this memoir to his

granddaughter Elinor," Rose says. "I marked some passages I'd like to read out to you."

"Was he the one who killed René?" Jacques asks.

"Yes, together with the main founder and leader of PRAC, Etienne Poupon," Annie replies while Rose looks for her glasses.

Jacques peers at her. "But why? What was their motive?"

"Your wealthy dad got wind from one of his connections that PRAC, the anti-capitalist party, was funded by the ultrarich Joel Gimbert." Annie turns to Monique. "I recall you telling us that Pierre-François objected to René's political activism."

"Very much so," Monique states. "They fought over it every time René came home for holidays."

Rose finds her glasses and puts them on. "We learned from the memoir that Pierre-François had relayed the scoop to René, hoping that René would be disgusted by their hypocrisy and quit PRAC."

"I'm assuming René confronted the PRAC leaders instead," Jacques says.

"He did. He gave them an ultimatum to return the tainted money or be exposed." Rose thumbs through to the first bookmarked page. "Here, Dany describes the first murder."

She reads it aloud.

We picked the lock and snuck in. I knew that René's room was the one on the left, and Grégoire's the one on the right. I'd been to their apartment that same morning, supposedly to discuss how Étienne and I were going to return the money to Joel Gimbert. But my real goal had been to scope the place, as Etienne and I planned René's murder.

Who could've predicted that René and Grégoire

would swap rooms later that day? My guess is the switch had something to do with Grégoire's and Bernadette's relationship becoming serious. Grégoire's room was too narrow to squeeze in a double bed if he was planning to get one.

Etienne and I tiptoed to what was now Grégoire's room. Unfortunately, Bernadette wasn't there that night. Even more unfortunately, Grégoire and René both had thick light brown hair trimmed in the same basic style. And the final coincidence that sealed Grégoire's fate was that he slept with his face to the wall that night. I pulled the pillow from under his head and muffled him while Étienne strangled him with a tie.

We realized our mistake only after he was dead. Etienne wanted to go to the other room and finish our business straight away. But I couldn't. I felt so sick I ran out and puked outside. And then I just couldn't make myself go back in. Not that night.

As Rose reads, there's keen attention, surprise, disbelief, and horror on the faces of the Chantomes family.

Rose finds the next passage and clears her throat.

The next day, after René discovered Grégoire's body, the police called him in for questioning. I received a call from Richard Frinnier, a childhood friend of mine who'd become a commissaire with the Paris Police Department. He told me that one of my fellow PRAC members was a suspect in a murder investigation. But I could rest easy, he reassured me. All the testimonies concurred that René and Grégoire had been on great terms. René had no motive to kill Gregoire. And again, according to all the witnesses, René would never kill another man, let alone a friend, in his sleep. The police weren't going to press charges.

It was after Richard's call that Étienne realized we could use our mistake to our advantage. All we had to do was give René a motive to kill Grégoire that didn't contradict his characterization by everybody else. An unrequited love for Bernadette was one such motive, making Grégoire's murder a crime of passion. René, being good, would naturally feel awful afterward and commit suicide as a penance for his crime.

Olivia's face contorts into a grimace of disgust. "Sick, cruel, despicable creatures! They revolt me."

"Add Richard Frinnier to that bunch," Annie says. "Dany had saved his life when they were kids, so he felt indebted. But it didn't bother him that he was accusing an innocent man of murder and covering up for the real murderers to repay his debt."

Monique's eyebrows raise. "Did Frinnier do those things?"

"Oh yes," Annie says. "As the lead investigator on Gregoire's case, he chose to go with Dany's and Etienne's fake testimonies, disregarding all the others. Later, that same Frinnier removed Dany's and Etienne's testimonies from the file."

"All to protect his murderous friend?" Hélène asks.

Annie wrinkles her nose. "And to cover up his own wrongdoing."

Rose lifts her eyes from the memoir. "Here's one more passage, if you're up for it."

We wore gloves. We planned and rehearsed every step. René had gotten lucky once, but this time we were leaving him no chance. Our only concern was that he wouldn't let us in, wary after what happened to Grégoire. But he did. He hadn't realized he'd been our target all along.

We pressed a chloroform-soaked cloth to his face, carried him to the bathroom and lowered him into the bathtub. I turned the hot water on. Etienne slashed René's wrists. While René bled out under Étienne's watchful eye, I found René's lecture notes and practiced just enough to write one short word—*Sorry*—on a blank sheet of paper.

We made sure to leave the note on René's desk, and the knife in the bathtub, before we left.

Someone around the table begins to weep. To Annie's surprise it isn't a female voice. She turns in the direction of the sobbing. It's Jacques.

Monique gets up and rounds the table, while he rises to his feet. They hug.

"It's all right," she says to him softly. "It's all right, honey."

Armand bangs his fist on the table. "Good thing Dany is dead! I could murder that piece of shit."

"And his buddy Etienne, too," Olivia chimes in.

Rose sizes them up over her glasses. "I hope you mean it figuratively, children. Just in case, let me read you one more passage, very brief. The final words of Dany's memoir."

She reopens the document in her hands.

Etienne and I did what we did to protect our secret. We had convinced ourselves that PRAC had the potential to change the country and the entire world for the better. We kept talking about the greater good. "The end justifies the means," we kept telling ourselves. I have come to see that we were wrong. It does not.

Twenty minutes later, Annie and her friends step out of the teahouse. The sun is still shining in the spotless sky. Annie smiles, her heart full. Everything is more beautiful, more enjoyable, more satisfying.

She has set the record straight. She has honored René's memory. Also, as an unexpected but delightful by-product, she has reconciled two siblings after a decades-long rift.

She has broken the goblin's spell and brought her Kai home.

Annie knows she will live the time she has left in that coveted state of mind that Rose calls by a fancy Buddhist name. The more common term works just as well, though.

*Inner peace.*

# AUTHOR'S NOTE

Like all my books, this one, too, blends fact and fiction, real locations, made-up places, historical figures, and invented characters. If you are curious to know which is which, then read on!

Les Tonneaux, the Chantomes' hotel in Le Crotoy is inspired by the hotel Les Tourelles in the same town. It's just as lovely and offers an amazing view of the Bay of the Somme.

The seaside town of Le Crotoy and the little steam train are real. I highly recommend both.

The retired mobster Napoleon "Big Napo" Albertini is a fictional character. His story is loosely based on a memoir by a former French Connection member Jean-Pierre Hernandez, alias Gros Pierrot. (*Quand j'étais gangster*, Flammarion, 2014).

The French Connection was a powerful organized crime syndicate that specialized in heroin trafficking. It operated out of Marseilles between the late 1930s and early 1970s. The story of its collaboration with the French secret services in the 1950s is based on facts with a few fictional characters such as Big Napo and the Leoni brothers, modeled on the Guerini brothers, thrown in.

Dear Reader,

I hope you enjoyed this novel! please **leave a review on Amazon** to help others discover my work.

If you haven't read any other Julie Cavallo mysteries yet, here's a sneak peek at book 1, "The Murderous Macaron" (Chanticleer MYSTERY & MAYHEM winner).

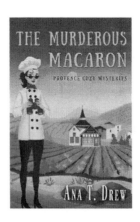

Julie has her freedom,
a dream job as a pastry chef,
and a corpse growing cold on her floor...

**Welcome to Beldoc, a small town in the heart of**

**Provence, imbued with lavender and fresh baked bread! You can idle around, or you can puzzle out a murder mystery.**

When a man dies on her watch in her pâtisserie, newly divorced chef Julie Cavallo is dismayed.

It isn't that she's a suspect.

The local gendarmerie captain signs off the death as a natural event. A heart attack.

But for a reason she won't discuss, Julie suspects Maurice Sauve was poisoned.

What's a girl to do?

She'll ignore the risk and seek justice for Maurice on her own!

Well, not quite on her own. Julie's eccentric grandmother, her snarky sister and her geeky sous chef are keen to help.

The team's amateurism is a challenge.

But there's also the pesky matter of no evidence, no clues, and soon, no body.

The murder—if it was a murder—was planned and executed flawlessly.

*Can a small-town baker solve the perfect crime?*

# ABOUT THE AUTHOR

Ana T. Drew is the evil mastermind behind the recent series of murders in the fictional French town of Beldoc.

When she is not writing cozy mysteries or doing mom-and-wife things, she can be found watching "The Rookie" to help her get over "Castle".

She lives in Paris but her heart is in Provence.

Website: ana-drew.com

a  amazon.com/author/ana-drew

g  goodreads.com/anadrew

BB  bookbub.com/authors/ana-t-drew

X  x.com/AnaTDrew

f  facebook.com/AnaDrewAuthor

ALSO BY ANA T. DREW

THE **JULIE CAVALLO INVESTIGATES** SERIES

The Murderous Macaron

Pastry chef Julie Cavallo has her freedom, her shop, and a corpse growing cold on her floor...

The Killer Karma

Julie unmasked a killer. Life is good once again... until her sous chef becomes a murder suspect.

The Sinister Superyacht

A luxury yacht. A tricky murder. An unlikely sleuth.

The Shady Chateau

Beware, dressing up as Napoleon can get you killed!

The Perils of Paris

When someone tries to kill her sister, it's time for Julie Cavallo to don her sleuthing cap

The Bloodthirsty Bee

It's springtime in Provence! Trees are in bloom and critters are abuzz — including a murderer or two.

The Deadly Donut

As bodies pile up in a luxury hotel, pastry chef Julie has precious little time to find the killer!

## Christmas Specials

The Canceled Christmas (novella)

Mayor Victor Jacquet receives a mystifying note. And then his small town mounts a rebellion...

An (un)Orthodox Christmas (novella)

Some believers observe Christmas in January. Some cops work homicide at that time...

The Twelve Suspects of Christmas (full-length novel)

Grannies, gangsters, murders—and a rollicking journey across France!

# EXCERPT FROM "THE MURDEROUS MACARON"

## JULIE CAVALLO INVESTIGATES, BOOK 1

"People drop dead on strangers all the time." Flo gives me an emphatic look. "Stop sulking, it's bad for business. Life goes on, Julie!"

At that, she waves and exits the shop.

Heeding my younger sister's questionable pep talk, I pick up a box of pistachio macarons and begin to gift wrap it.

The front door chimes, announcing a new customer.

I force the corners of my mouth upward in what I hope resembles a professional smile. But my face lengthens again when I realize who's entering the shop. The man in the doorway isn't a customer. He's a cop, Capitaine Gabriel Adinian of the Beldoc Gendarmerie. The one who's looking into the death of Maurice Sauve.

I hug myself, as a sudden shiver runs through my body on this balmy June afternoon.

*That poor man!*

To go so quickly and irreversibly, and at the worst possible time! Not just from my perspective, even though I can't deny I'd rather he suffered his heart attack before or after my macaron-making class. On a less selfish note, the timing was unfortunate for Maurice himself. When I asked everyone at the beginning of the workshop to tell the class about themselves, he said he'd been through a prolonged midlife crisis and had finally glimpsed the light at the end of the tunnel.

He said he'd embarked on a quest for a purpose to his life after realizing two years back that sorting mail at the post office wasn't it. A year of volunteering with the Red Cross in Southeast Asia convinced him that charity work wasn't it either. Back in Beldoc, he dipped a toe into all sorts of things from music to stock trading. Recently, he discovered baking.

I remember him gushing as he concluded his introduction: "I have a really good feeling about this!"

Twenty minutes later, he grimaced, collapsed to the floor, and died.

I shudder and rub my arms.

As Capitaine Adinian draws nearer, I train my gaze on his face. His features are highly irregular. In theory, no woman would find him handsome unless she'd been studying iguanas on a deserted island for a year.

In actuality, the matter of his attractiveness is less straightforward.

The overall structure of his face makes up for the flaws of his individual features. His prominent nose and mouth match the angular firmness of his jawline, which his three-day-old stubble cannot hide. His dark brown eyes reel you in. He gives off an aura of effortless, natural virility.

*Chill out, Julie.*

It's just a visceral reaction of a thirty-year-old woman to a guy she finds hot. It'll pass in a moment. Besides, I don't find him hot. And, recalling his attitude during our first encounter last night, I don't even like him.

Capitaine Adinian halts across the counter from me.

A thought crosses my mind. What if this isn't about

Maurice Sauve? What if he's come here with the aim of purchasing an assortment of my confections?

*Ha-ha.* That was the most ridiculous of all the ridiculous ideas I've ever had. And, trust me, I've had many.

Adinian surveys me, muttering something unintelligible under his breath.

I choose to interpret it as "Good morning, Madame Cavallo" and not "You didn't think I was done with you, eh".

The latter option is more likely though. I'm sure Flo would agree. My little sis likes to say that if you keep mentally photoshopping the ugly truth out of people, you'll surround yourself with friends you can always rely on to backstab you. At twenty-two, she's full of acerbic wisdom, aka snark, that she dishes out to all and sundry.

"Julie's Gluten-Free Delights," Adinian says, quoting the sign above the entrance. "But here in Beldoc, we like our gluten."

Is that his idea of a friendly icebreaker? The butterflies in my stomach calm down, as he confirms that he's exactly who I think he is. A discourteous hick.

"I may have lived in Paris half my life"—I look him directly in the eye—"but I'm a Beldocian like you. You'd be surprised how many residents are gluten-intolerant or gluten-sensitive."

Personally, I'm neither. But for the sake of coherence, I stopped consuming wheat-based food the moment I decided to launch a gluten-free bakery.

"Of course," Adinian deadpans.

And then he looks left and right, as if trying to figure out where all those gluten-free buffs might be hiding in my empty shop.

*The cheek of him!*

I wish Rose was here this morning! She'd flip back her perfect silver bob and arch a masterfully shaped eyebrow.

"What happened to good manners, young man?" she'd say in her most la-di-da tone of voice while staring him down. My grandma might even tell him to step out and reenact his entry, politely this time.

And you know what? He just might do it. There's something about Rose that compels people, pets, and potted plants to indulge her.

Eric steps out of the kitchen. "The vanilla macaron shells are ready, Chef. Want to check before I stick them in the oven?"

"No, that's fine, go ahead," I say to my sous chef before turning back to Capitaine Adinian.

"We're going to conclude natural death," Adinian says, skipping any form of transition.

I give him a small nod.

"Monsieur Sauve's family said he'd been under a lot of stress over the last two years," he adds. "Too much beer, too little exercise. They had feared he'd end up with a heart attack."

"His *family*?" I was under the impression Maurice Sauve was single. Then again, he never said as much.

Adinian puts his elbow on the counter. "He had a cousin living on the same street."

"I see."

He half-turns toward the door, then scratches the back of his head, and turns toward me again. "Can you recount last evening's events again, everything you remember?"

"Er... again? Why?" The prospect of reliving those moments doesn't appeal to me at all. "Didn't you just say there wasn't any foul play involved?"

"It's just formality. I'm finishing my report, and I want to make sure I have all the details right."

My shoulders slump. "OK."

He heads toward the sitting area, plonks himself down

into a vintage bistro chair, and points to another chair. "Have a seat."

*Making ourselves at home, are we?*

Trying not to show my irritation, I sit down across a round table from him and begin my sad tale of yesterday's macaron-making workshop that didn't go as planned.

He listens, barely taking any notes.

When I get to the part where I asked my students to mix the ingredients I'd prepared for them, Capitaine Adinian leans forward. "Who prepared and laid out the ingredients?"

"I did."

"When?"

"Shortly before the class began."

"Did you leave the shop, even for a brief time, after you had everything ready for the class?" he asks.

"No."

He scribbles something in his little notebook. "Please continue."

"Most participants struggled to get their batter to stiffen," I say. "Some gave up, claiming it was impossible without an electric mixer."

"Did Maurice Sauve give up?"

"Quite the contrary. He whisked unrelentingly, switching hands but never pausing. He was the first to complete the task."

Capitaine Adinian writes that down.

"I gave him one of these." I show Adinian the remaining badges that Flo had made for the workshop.

"Great Baking Potential," he reads aloud.

"Then I went around with his bowl and had everyone admire the perfect consistency of the batter."

"Did anything stand out or seem unusual at that point?"

I gaze up at the ceiling, picturing the scene of me praising Maurice Sauve's firm, satiny batter, students giving him their thumbs-up, and him smiling, visibly stoked. But he isn't just smiling, he's also... Panic squeezing my throat, I zero in on his face. He's panting.

*Oh. My. God.*

I clap my hand over my mouth. "What if he'd whisked too hard? What if that exertion caused his heart attack?"

"Only an intense workout, especially at freezing temperatures, can trigger a heart attack," Adinian says.

"He whisked intensely."

"Madame Cavallo, I've never heard of anyone whisking themselves to an early grave."

## *End of Excerpt*

Printed in Great Britain
by Amazon

34820916R00142